# DEATH HEARS A
## *Siren*

### NORMA'S CLEANING SERVICE
### BOOK 2

# ELIZABETH GUIZZETTI

For permission requests, email the publisher, with the subject line
"Permissions" to Elizabeth@zbpublications.com

Cover and Interior Illustrations by Elizabeth Guizzetti

This is a work of fiction. Names, characters, businesses, places,
events and incidents are products of the author's imagination or
used in a fictitious manner. Any resemblance to actual persons,
living or dead, or actual events is purely coincidental.

Printed in the United States of America

Paperback ISBN-13: 978-1-950708-28-4
Ebook ISBN-13: 978-1-950708-29-1

Dedicated to all those who believe in love
even though this book
(and lots of other murder mysteries)
often expose unhappy relationships.

Keep on Believing!

# Dear Readers:

MAKE NO MISTAKE; THIS IS ANOTHER COZY murder mystery about vampires. This story also hints at the struggles of witches and merpeople in modern Seattle. *Death Hears a Siren* is the second book in *Norma Cleaning Service*. Like the other books in this series, these books do not have sex or swearing on the page.

Norma Mae Rollins and Carlos Fisher-Perez first appeared as secondary characters in *Immortal House*, 2018. This is the Second Edition of *Death Hears a Siren*. Not much has changed except a round of editing and some changes in the illustrations. The biggest major change is the book is now written in the first person. As I said in the foreword of *Death Pulls a Stake Out*, I made the change so all the future books in the series are told from the same point of view.

As I have been writing the last three *Norma's Cleaning Service*, plus a "how Norma and Carlos met" prequel, I struggled with the POV issue which is why I am releasing second editions written from first person.

If you want to read about Norma's childhood with Bill and Derrik, you can read the stand-alone novel, *Accident Among Vampires or What Would Dracula Do?*, 2021.

I hope you enjoy Norma's second book.

-Elizabeth

September 29, 2019

# Chapter 1

## 7:00 PM

WIND WHIPPED MY PONYTAIL AND tangled my sweaty curls as I carried the box of my client's personal belongings. People who didn't live in Seattle assumed September was rainy. Though it was autumn, as global warming worsened, September was decidedly dry and chilly at night. Though the burn bans had been lifted from the state, the bad air from summer forest fires still lingered.

The boxes filled with costumes, props, and bedding were unwieldy in my slender arms but not particularly heavy. Like all vampires, I had slowly grown stronger with time. I figured after sixty-eight years as a vampire, I had the strength of three fourteen-year-old farm girls—since a fourteen-year-old farm girl is what I had been on the night I was changed.

Still, my only employee and closest friend, Carlos Fisher Perez, carried three boxes to my one. Before his first death, he was a luchador in his prime. After an injury put his wrestling career on hold, he took some questionable medical advice and a potion from a werewolf Shaman. Now a shade (also called a zombie), he walked the Earth until his soul freed itself. Carlos and I both wanted that to happen later rather than sooner. Vampires had lots of rules, and I liked having a nonjudgmental friend. Carlos had three cute little cats which he adored. Though his body was slowly putrefying, he claimed that he, too, was growing stronger than he had been in life. (However, he kept healthy with daily Crossfit, a low carb diet, and the occasional body part from a corpse.)

"Oh, do be careful, Sir." Atmospheric mist swirled around our client, Pamela. She floated above the middle bench seat as she eyed Carlos's slow, uneven gait.

Carlos couldn't answer. His vocal cords were crushed in the accident that ultimately took his life. He slid the two boxes of dresses and a dishpack into the van, but his deep brown eyes were filled with a storm. He was annoyed.

"Carlos is very strong; he won't drop anything," I assured our client as I pulled at my shirt to unstick it from my back.

"Oh, I'm sure he won't," Pamela said in a voice that betrayed she was sure he might.

I pushed the boxes to their places in the van, organized for easy removal. I jumped back out and went inside the building to make sure we hadn't miss anything.

Norma's Cleaning Service was initially a service for vampires when hunting got a little messy—and we still did clean-ups—but I didn't balk at any paying job. We ran all types of errands for the supernatural community and any humans the world ignored.

Since ghosts moved more languidly than other species and took such a comparative time to move a single physical object, Pamela needed help transporting her things to the small, still mostly rural, city of Carnation for a job to haunt a corn maze, pumpkin patch and connected bed and breakfast.

Pamela had existed in Seattle since the 1880s. She didn't want to leave, but her former diner was slated for demolition to make room for a high-rise tower. She had sought other employment in the city, but most people didn't want to live in haunted condos anymore. Every one was so concerned with property values. Seattle was just too expensive for ghosts.

"Want to drive tonight?" I asked as I secured the last box.

Carlos nodded.

"You okay?"

Carlos wrote: **Just annoyed with this crap job. Also hungry.**

"Sorry. I've broccoli in the car."

Carlos: **Good.**

I wondered if anything else was wrong. I hoped he wasn't decomposing again. Perhaps, there was something else I could do for Carlos, but other than paying a fair wage and full medical, I didn't know what that would be. Besides the members of my vampire family, Carlos was my only friend. I hated the thought that I would continue to exist after he was gone.

ONCE CARLOS CONSUMED A POUND OF broccoli and passed the cities of Seattle and Bellevue, his normal good mood resurfaced.

Each time I crossed Lake Washington, my mother's sheep farm called to me though it had been long closed and turned into a Christmas Tree Farm. So did the land where I was transformed.

Still, I chatted with Pamela quietly and ignored the whispers. Small talk helped distract me from the dark loam which sang in the valley between Cougar and Tiger Mountains, where I had been born as a human and reborn as a vampire. I fought the urge to ask Carlos to stop so I might return to the Earth of my homeland by reminding myself that we had a client. When that didn't work, I reminded myself my hometown of Issaquah had exploded in size since I was really a girl. Mom was long dead. As was my creator. Issaquah might have been my hometown, but Seattle was home.

Sparkling lights dotted the sides of Cougar and Tiger mountains. My eyes followed I-90 as it stretched east, deeper into the Cascades, where King County was still pastoral.

We turned off the interstate and headed north on Preston-Fall City Road. Every mile away from the mountain, the call grew weaker and allowed me to regain focus on the job.

The new Victorian-style bed and breakfast looked to be a first-class experience. I hoped Pamela would enjoy haunting it. The hosts, a middle-aged married couple, their cat, dogs, and a menagerie of rabbits, seemed pleasant enough and excited to have a ghost working for them. The humans even helped unpack the van.

"So you're undead too," the first host asked.

"Ever consider show business?" her wife completed the thought.

"No," I lied.

Carlos typed and made his phone read aloud: **Did it**

once before. Norma pays better.

My entire experience was show business—just the business of making the supernatural community disappear. I gave the hosts a flyer; I accepted one of theirs. "We clean up all kinds of messes and run errands for the supernatural community."

He helped Pamela hang up her collection of white, tattered Victorian gowns. Pamela often wore physical dresses, so unbelieving eyes could more easily see her.

As we were leaving, the first host offered us free tickets to the corn maze and two bright orange pumpkins. "They'll last if you don't carve them until a week or so before Halloween."

Carlos gave them a nod as he jumped in the driver's seat. I thanked the hosts and set the B&B information in my backseat organizer. I liked to keep track of all businesses which at least dabbled in the supernatural community. Who knew when they might need something professionally cleaned?

It was nearly midnight before we were back on the road to Seattle. The dark forests of Tiger Mountain called, stronger this time since the van headed directly towards its eastern slopes. Its call would be loudest once we passed the valley. I understood Pamela's concern about leaving any of her possessions in Seattle.

"Mind if we stop? I got some meat in the cooler."

Carlos: **Barbecue?**

"Heck yeah."

Carlos hit on the turn signal and changed lanes toward the right when an unknown number rang on my cellphone through the Bluetooth system. He grunted out a sound that meant damn.

I tapped the screen to answer: "Norma's Cleaning Service."

"Your flyer says you clean up all kinds of messes, and you don't ask questions." A woman's voice clipped with an east coast accent said in a cross between a statement and question.

Carlos turned off the turn signal and continued westward. He knocked on the dash. It was a private signal between them. **Be on guard.**

"I ask what I need to ask," I carefully adjusted my tone to firm and proficient.

"My coven sisters are renting a houseboat and found a siren in the living room."

"Coven sisters? Are you vampires?"

"No. Witches... Why would vampires stay in a houseboat? I thought water stole all vampire power."

"Only holy water," I lied to keep up the myth. "Not lake water."

Carlos laughed as he always did when someone asked about the supposed vampire myths. I figured some European vampires from landlocked countries couldn't swim and started all the water-based tales. However, I spent my childhood playing in streams and swimming in lakes and Puget Sound, both as a human and vampire.

"I saw this movie where a shower killed a vampire," the voice said.

"*Daughters of Darkness*?" A movie buff, I loved horror films. "1971: Lesbian vampires meet an abusive jerk and his pretty wife."

"I think so?..." The woman's voice wavered.

"It's a good flick, but I shower every day," I said. "So, where are you?"

"On Lake Union."

"What marina?"

The witch gave the address.

"How many are with you?"

"Two. Three, including me."

"Your name?" I asked.

"You need my name?"

We usually charged $4000 for basic cleanings, but beside me, Carlos put out his palm with all five fingers spread. The website listed the price of Deep Cleanings at $4000 to $6000 plus unusual expenses, so the price wasn't unheard of.

"Unless you plan to pay cash, and I'll want to see the cash upfront, mermaid disposal starts at $5000, plus any additional expenses," I said.

Carlos gave a thumbs-up.

"My name is Bianca Townsend. My sisters and I planned to put split the cost with our credit cards. Is that okay?"

"Yep. That will be fine." I checked the GPS for traffic updates. "We'll be there in twenty."

I hit the touch screen to end the call before Bianca said anything else.

Carlos touched the screen, which played one of his prerecorded messages: **Something about the client's voice told me they'd be a pain.**

"I hear that." I gazed out the window at the familiar darkness pierced by urban sprawl.

Since I watched so many movies, Carlos also prerecorded: **That movie good?**

"*Daughters of Darkness*? I guess. Probably not your thing.

"It's European. Lots of long shots and talking. Beautifully filmed. But, Derrik fast-forwarded through the scene where the husband abused his wife. He told me to cover my eyes—and I was like forty—so it must have gotten pretty bad. But the rest of the movie was okay."

Carlos: **Not sold.**

Carlos enjoyed a casual friendship with the vampire, Derrik Miller, who created my creator, William T. Caruso. After the coven discovered Bill's criminal activities and failing mental health, he took me into his home to raise me. While physically, I could not mature past fourteen, I was able to become, as Derrik used to say, an accomplished, well-read young lady.

Over the past decades, Derrik has watched plenty of science fiction, horror, and mystery movies with me. However, he prefers a good farce or romantic comedy.

And so does Carlos.

September 30, 2019

# Chapter 2

## Midnight

THE HOUSEBOAT WAS SUPER CUTE IN Seahawks green and blue with natural cedar trim. The slip was squeezed between two equally cute houseboats painted in fun themed colors. The second deck was a covered patio with white plastic furniture arranged in a way that I guessed there must be a view of Gasworks Park.

Carlos texted: **The owner must make bank.**

"Yeah. I should think so."

The wind blowing off the water cooled us from our previous job. This late, the only traffic noise was the large trucks delivering goods to Seattle's stores or crossing the city over the highway. If I closed my eyes, it might seem as if Seattle had a few hundred thousand fewer people just as it once did, decades before.

I filled my lungs with the cool autumn air. Though I did not need to breathe air, I still did. Most vampires who worked with the living pretended to be alive, and I was no different in that regard. Plus I liked breathing.

The sound of the gentle lake currents lapping against the dock would have made for a perfect night if not for the scent of death emanating from the houseboat.

All the windows glowed through the curtains from the light within. No doubt the witches wanted the lights on after finding a body.

"You're Norma?" A shorter than average, slightly round Black woman opened the front door even before we made it down the slip. She held a purple clutch monogrammed with a G in front of her like a shield which matched the purple flowers on the sundress. Her clammy right hand clasped mine in an abbreviated handshake. "You look so...young."

"I'm older than I look," I said. "And you are?"

Her dark eyes widened. "Yes. You're a vampire, right? We got your number from the local witch coven."

"Yes, and my associate, Carlos Fisher-Perez. And what is your name?"

"Oh sorry, Gwenna Harris."

"What coven are you members of?"

She mentioned a well-known coven based out of New York. Gwenna, who I guessed was in her late thirties by her clothes and mannerisms, chewed on the inside of her cheek as she blocked our entrance. Her arms crossed in under her breasts and then she put her hands in her pockets and then as if the position displeased her, she crossed her arms again. I hoped dead sirens weren't an everyday occurrence for the woman and Gwenna really was just flustered. However, in the back of my mind, I considered that she might be pretending.

"What are you?" Gwenna said to Carlos.

Carlos scribbled on his notepad: An annoyed shade.

"What's a shade?"

Zombie.

"May we see your mess?" I asked and wondered if I

needed to give Carlos a pain-in-the-rear client bonus.

"Oh, yes. Sorry." The woman stepped aside.

The long body of a siren (also known as a mermaid or a daughter of Poseidon) was sprawled across the houseboat's tiled living room. Her spines had sliced open the side of a chair, and there was a long scratch against the wooden coffee table. It looked like she fell. Up close, her neck was bruised.

The other two witches stood in the kitchen, watching with large wine goblets in hand. Gwenna went over to them and poured herself a glass of wine in a lipstick smudged glass. They were all three beautiful women, but very different looking.

Bianca's name fit her coloring. She was white, probably in her late forties, her lips were subtly pink, her hair only a few shades darker than her flesh. Her blue eyes rested upon me. She wrinkled her nose and cocked her head. She was either drunk or so wealthy she could afford a body dump.

"Did any of you know her?" I asked.

"No." Bianca opened her purse and pulled out a credit card. "How do you know it is a her?"

"In general, the same way you tell on a human or vampire."

"Which is?"

"Mostly the tattoos. However, this one by her size and enlarged breasts. She has had and breastfed children. Males of this species tend to be larger and have more defined muscles and wider shoulders. I've worked with sirens several times."

"Oh. We've never seen a siren up close before. Look at those claws."

The webbed fingers of merfolk ended with sharp talons which evolved to grab animals off the shore and quickly rip into their prey.

"Do they really sing to lure sailors to their death?" Gwenna asked.

"They are great singers, but they sing for their own pleasure, not to kill humans. You know how stories are. Some idiot probably heard a siren and crashed his boat—next thing you know it's the siren's fault."

The witches laughed.

I took the card in hand and realized I could not read their minds. I was used to blocking my mind so I wasn't overwhelmed, but also receiving random thoughts or emotions from people. Standing in front of three people I couldn't read at all was a shock. I would never show disconcertment to a client. "So three ways: even split?"

"Yes."

Still nothing. The emptiness of their minds gave me bad vibes, but I didn't want to fall into tired witch stereotypes. I had worked for plenty of vampires and witches who knew I could read minds and hid their thoughts appropriately before. But these were new clients.

*If Bianca liked vampire movies as much as I do, she probably figured all vampires could read minds and arranged appropriately.*

I texted Carlos. **They casted some sort of dampening spell in here. I can't read their minds.**

Carlos: **Want to bail?**

Me: **Just wanted you to know.**

"Some vacation this turned out to be." Bianca pouted

and took another gulp of wine. "I originally planned to hire a stripper. Instead, we hired you to clean up this mess. I don't suppose we could get you to take off your clothes?" She gestured at Carlos, who was writing out the receipts.

He growled. His former job as a wrestler ensured he was incredibly fit. However, he hated when people flirted with him when on the job.

"Just asking."

"Shut your damn mouth, Madam," I said. "He is not above eating clients who annoy us."

Gwenna handed over her credit card next. She seemed relieved by the action. "Forgive my sister, Sir. She is a little drunk."

The final witch, Medea Fotos, was another white woman with long dark hair that she kept pinned in a bun. Since she didn't wear cosmetics, she looked older than Bianca, but I guessed she was actually a little younger. Though Gwenna had seemed rattled and Bianca was sloshed, Medea seemed the most nervous. Her eyes glanced out the window every few moments. Her voice cracked; her chin trembled. "Thank you for coming. We appreciate all the work you do—keeping our community safe."

"You're welcome. Excuse me; I need to get my mop," I said.

Medea opened a pantry door. "Cleaning supplies are in here."

"Thanks, but I'll use my own stuff, so all evidence gone with me."

"Of course! How clever." Medea glanced out the window again.

Wondering if Medea had runs in with the children of Poseidon before, I returned to the van to get a mop and bucket and extra thick body bag and a handful of corks. "It's just a cleanup," I muttered, but somewhere deep in my stomach, I didn't believe it.

The poor child of Poseidon might have come in here to die. Whales beached themselves, why not the merfolk? With climate change and acidification of Earth's oceans, many merfolk suffered from new sicknesses—or ancient ones they no longer had immunity. My coven brother, Ryan Jones, was a marine biologist. I wished for his insight.

As I reentered the houseboat, I heard splashing in the darkness of the deep lake. Humans wouldn't be playing fetch with their dogs at this hour. I stared over the water, trying to see if anything slipped upon the small wavelets. Though vampire sight is good in the dark, I could not through the black water of Lake Union. *Let it be sea lions.*

Using my camera, I took several photos. There was almost no blood underneath the body, though there were slices along the torso and throat of the mermaid. I had cleaned up lots of messes. There was often a lot more blood when someone was feeding or fighting. If I had to guess, it looked like the poor woman was strangled to death, unless she had died of sickness. The merwoman's body was in incomplete rigor mortis, not completely stiff. I saw no rot, but her green eyes were already clouding over.

Across the mermaid's shoulders and tale, she wore her community and family tattoos. Her personal tattoos across her chest as was common. I recognized the symbols from the pod off the shore of Golden Gardens. I had worked for several members of that group before. The mermaid was a local.

Carlos lifted the body carefully. He placed corks on the stiff spines along her long silvery tail, so she didn't puncture the body bag and slice open his arms. I cleaned up what little mermaid's blood had spilled on the tile floor, taking special care among the grout.

I sewed the slash in the upholstery. Using wood filler, I repaired the table, then polishhed used a high quality furniture wax. Once waxed, the scratch was nearly invisible. I vacuumed the living room rug and washed the handprint off the sliding glass door to ensure the houseboat would look as good as new. "Was the mess anywhere else in the houseboat?" I asked.

"I don't think so. Our bags are how we left them. Even my jewelry has not been touched." Bianca studied my work.

"Do you want me to fill the scratch a little more?" I asked.

"No, I can't even see it. You really are quite good."

"Thank you."

Norma's Cleaning Service was well informed about the rites of the different species. We would drive through Fremont into Ballard towards Golden Gardens. We would unwrap the poor woman's body onto the sand, remove the corks and adorn her scalp with sea kelp. Then we would wade into the water and allow the unnamed mermaid's body to drift into the Sound. Her soul would be at rest with her people. Or, at least, that had been the plan until an otherworldly voice shattered the night and echoed through the living room.

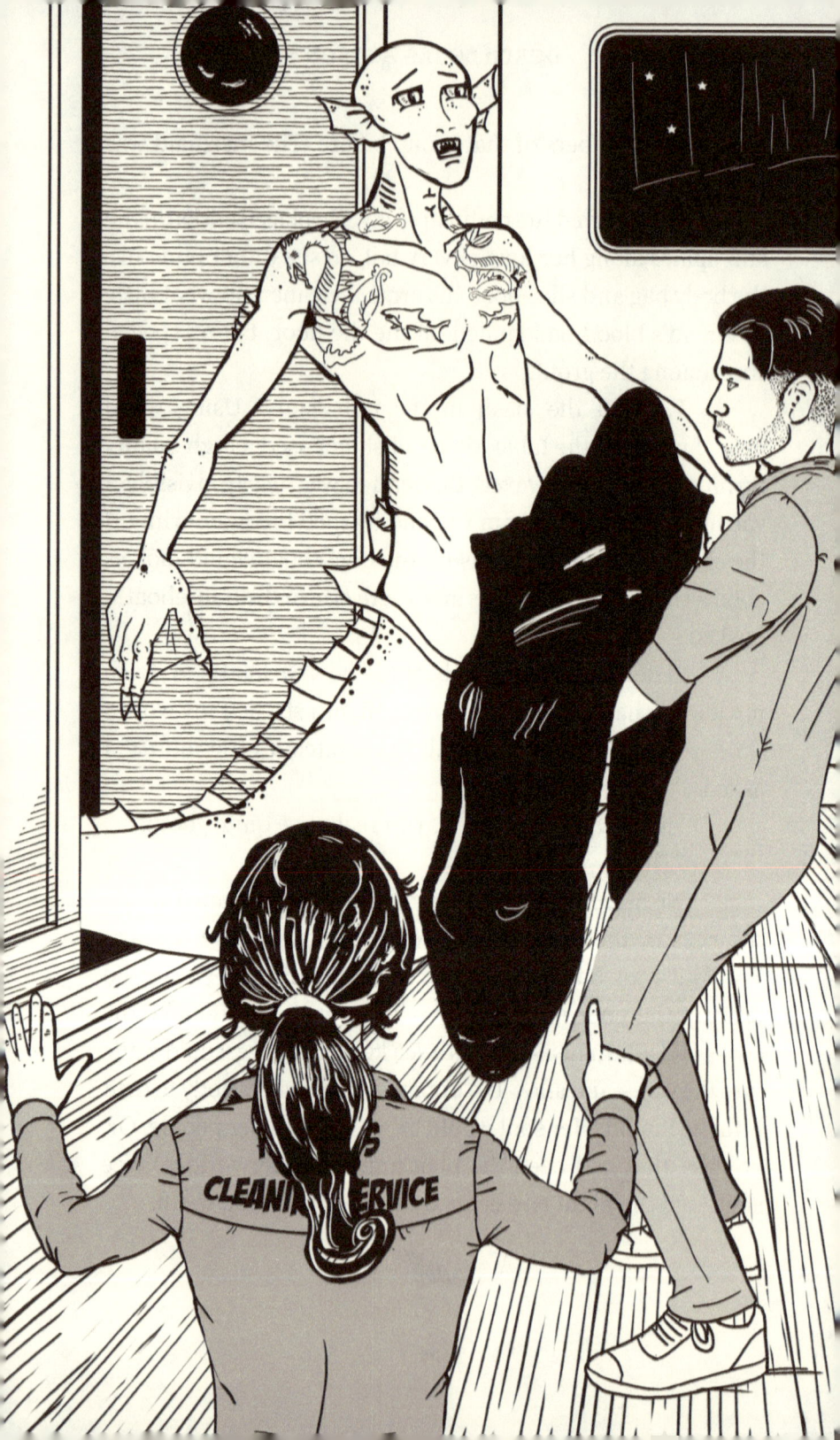

# Chapter 3

## 3:17 AM

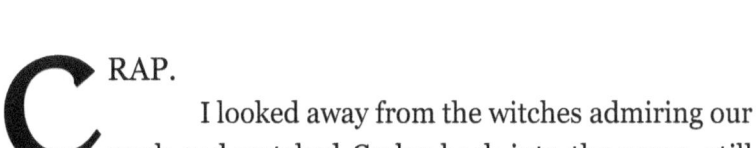

**C**RAP.

I looked away from the witches admiring our work and watched Carlos back into the room, still holding the body bag.

His expression meant only one thing: **Danger.**

Sleek and muscular merfolk pulled themselves through the door, three males and a female. Their faces set in masks of rage. Wiry arms hauled their lower half which sparkled and undulated liked a snake on dry land. While merfolk didn't look kindly on merfolk who went around drowning less capable swimmers such as vampires, they looked even less likely kindly on those who harmed their people. The first one through the door reached for Carlos, who jumped out of the way of the clawed webbed hand.

He gently set down the body bag onto the tiled floor. He backed slowly away from it; his palms outstretched and empty.

The witches screamed as houseboat grew crowded. Yet, I could only sense their deepest fear, not any thoughts. As a true telepath, I was more terrified by my lack of insight than the merfolk's claws.

One of merman cried, "Zaria!"

Even his sobs sounded musical. His wails filled the room as he fell upon the body bag. His posture covered his community tattoos, but I noticed the sea serpent snaking up his left arm and down his right. Between that serpent's coils was the mark of the Southern Pod and his marriage mark to the Golden Gardens Pod.

The merfolk balanced on their tails, standing at their full height, they towered over me. The three mermen were approximately a half meter longer than an average adult vampire (or human) male was tall. The female was slightly shorter but not by much. Their muscular bodies glittered in beautiful iridescent shades of algae green, and their chests were covered in spectacular tattoos.

"Can you identify the body?" I asked.

"My wife...my wife."

The body bag was still closed.

"Are you trying to say your wife is missing?"

The other two men reached for the man and pulled him off the body bag. I recognized one: Samuel Poseidonson was a former client. (Poseidonchild, Poseidondottier, or Poseidonson were a merperson's public name. Their private surnames were only used in their community. However, vampires didn't have private surnames.)

"I am Norma Rollins of Norma's Cleaning Service. My associate and I were called in for a cleanup. As your kinfolk know, I do this job no questions asked for all species which walk or swim on this Earth.

"Hello Samuel, I would have like to meet again in better circumstances."

His tearful eyes focused on me. "Has Zaria..."

The third man shouted. "What are you doing with our kinswoman's body?"

"I work no questions asked," I said in a calm, clear voice.

"Yeah, I know." Samuel said, "Irving lay off."

With my hands raised and palms out, I said, "First, we do not know whose body this is. Can one of you tell me if this is your missing Zaria?"

The male who had wept over the bodybag slithered closer to the witches who huddled together in the kitchen, behind the breakfast bar. One of the witches screamed as he swung around and his dorsal fin entered the kitchen. I thought about telling them to shut up. I stepped between them.

It didn't help because Bianca snapped, "Get lost, this is private property, and you weren't invited here."

His thick muscular arms covered in tattoos were impressive. I guessed he was about forty—somewhere between young and old. "This is my private property. My wife is your host."

"We found her on the floor," Gwenna said, quickly peeking over the bar. "We called our coven sisters. They gave us Norma's number."

"Then how did you get in?" His shout echoed through the rooms, but I noticed his strange posture, as straight as a statue. He was either enraged or strangely relieved, but I couldn't read his mind. I wondered if I focused, I might open his mind, but I didn't want to take my attention off the one they called Irving, with his claws ten inches from my face.

I normally could read the children of Poseidon quite easily, whatever spell the witches had cast was quite powerful. It must be some sort of spacial field dulling my insight.

"Get in?" Bianca asked. "Through the front door."

"My cousin owns this houseboat," Samuel said. "And she always hands off the keys to her guests. She was alive earlier today."

"We knew something was wrong when Zaria wasn't singing for the moon as is our people's custom," the Poseidondottier said.

I stepped closer to Zaria's husband, ready to get toe to fin with the mermen, if need be. "First, look at this body and ensure it is your kinswoman, if you please?"

"I will look," he said, his haunting voice barely above a whisper.

I unzipped the bag.

He dropped his eyes at the bruised face. "It is her. Which one of you destroyed our happy redd?" (Redd is the common name of a merfolk's home or a salmon's nest.)

His clawed hands covered his face and his shoulders shook. "We have nine children. Now they don't have a mother. Which one of you did this?"

Samuel put his arm around Zaria's husband.

Stepping closer, I said with a soft voice, "Mr. Poseidonson, Sir, what is your name?"

"Kellen." The man lifted his head to look upon me; I he had no tears in his deep green eyes. Still, that didn't mean much. Over the long decades, plenty of times I saw those who stifled tears to a point in time which they might be alone.

"And you, Madam?"

"Lilianna, and that is my husband, Irving."

I reintroduced myself using short sentences in a clear speaking voice. "My name is Norma. This is Carlos. We are from Norma's Cleaning Service. How can we help you? We have wrapped the body of your dear wife and kinswoman for transport."

"You're supposed to get rid of the body." Bianca slapped the countertop.

"And I am. I would have given poor Zaria a proper burial, but if I can give the body to her kin, I will."

"Do we get a refund?" Medea asked.

"Hell no. You paid me to clean up this mess, and I am cleaning up this mess," I said.

"We paid you to clean the body no questions asked," Medea said.

Everyone started shouting over each other. Samuel slithered towards the bar, his webbed hands curling into tight fists. "If you don't give us answers, you will suffer a little drowning."

Gwenna shot off a small electric shock which raised the hair on my head. It hit a vase which shattered, causing a line of sharp ceramic bits to fall to the floor. (Another thing to clean up!)

The merfolk would have to glide across it to get to the witches. Gwenna might be a little scattered, but she could think quickly.

"I didn't have to miss. We didn't hurt anyone!"

"People always blame witches. No one ever blames the merfolk," Bianca said.

Carlos bone-chilling shout quieted the crowd. His

phone said aloud, **Shut your mouths when Norma speaks.**

Everyone glared at each other, but no one said another word when a well-built, muscular zombie told them what to do.

Someone pounded on the front door. A weathered male voice shouted: "Quiet down in there. We're trying to sleep. If I come over again, I'm calling the cops."

I apologized and told the voice, "I'll quiet everyone down."

The voice wandered away muttering about offsite owners doing short term rentals and how there should be a rule against it.

I didn't want to get into a major discussion right at this minute, but I thought about how many condo declarations had rules were which associations used to forbid short-term rentals, even if they weren't actually prohibiting short-term rentals. The Paper Flower Consortium required every thrall to sign a lease and to file said lease was $200 for the vampire. Houseboat slips at a privately-owned marina probably had different rules and I didn't know them.

"But we must know who killed my cousin!" Samuel cried. "Norma, Carlos will you help us?"

I pumped my palm up and down, hoping to keep people's voices down.

**Yes, but we'll need to be paid if we are going to be spending the rest of the night here.** Carlos said through his phone.

There was a subtle shift in the attitude in the room, but I still couldn't read from where.

"What about our vacation?" Bianca cried.

"What does she know? She's just a kid," Kellen said. "And he's a zombie."

"Thanks to Norma, that woman I told you about never bothered me again," Samuel eyed his cousin sharply. "Or is there a reason you don't want Norma to help us?"

I might not be able to read their minds, but I could read the animosity.

"I just want it done right," Kellen said.

"Well, Samuel is a satisfied customer. He is correct. I ensured the woman would never return to your redds after we got rid of her," I said.

"So you ate her after all?" Samuel asked. His dashing smile told me he wanted that to be the answer.

It wasn't, but Samuel's trust in me had to be justified. With practiced confidence and precision, I grinned and raised a single brow. "No, she was high as a kite, but I know some monsters who like to party."

Carlos's eyes were full of mirth as if he was ready to meet his final death by laughter. Outwardly, he growled in agreement. We had to keep our street cred. I glanced at Carlos and put five fingers on my arm.

His head bobbed once.

"We'll need 5000 dollars to figure out who solved the crime," I said.

"5000 dollars? What for?" Samuel said.

"I suggest you let us do an autopsy," I said quickly. "And you will have a solution before dawn."

"Not in here!" Bianca cried out. "We are on vacation!"

"More than that, we have to pay for damages to the houseboat," Medea said.

"The tile can be mopped again," I said to Kellen.

"You want to do an autopsy?" He asked with a flustered look on his face. "Or the zombie?"

"Neither of us. Let me call in my coven brother: Dr. Ryan Jones. He is a marine biologist and a great admirer of Poseidon's children."

The four merfolk spoke in their own language. Samuel pulled out his cell phone off his pocket and said something to Google. I didn't understand any of it—except they kept repeating Jones.

Samuel turned towards me. "This is Dr. Ryan Jones?"

He showed Ryan's last photo from the 1980s before he was transformed into a vampire. He used it as the author photograph on his one books. The light pinstripe suit, dark shirt, and pink tie looked straight out of Miami Vice.

"Yes."

"We remember this study—he wanted to help with the coming acidification of the oceans. He was concerned long before it came into the mainstream consciousness."

"Yes, that is correct," I said.

Poseidon's children went into conference again. The witches were also whispering to each other.

Finally, Samuel turned to me. "As you have treated me fairly in the past, we give our permission for an autopsy."

I texted Ryan.

No immediate answer.

Since I didn't have time to waste, I called our shared ancestor's office. As I assumed, Derrik's receptionist answered on the second ring. "Miller and Associates."

"Hi, Suzan, it's Norma. Is Derrik available?"

"Hold on, sweetie, lemme check."

She put the call through immediately.

"Good evening, Norma," Derrik said in the cool vampire way. His second question was not vampiric at all. "Are you in danger?"

"No, I need a marine biologist. Tell Ryan I'll pay him for an autopsy."

Her former guardian sighed. "Are you extending your services without appropriate legal and financial counsel?"

"Yes."

"You need to get a license for detective work—and your insurance will go up. It might affect your profit margin. It would be prudent if you run the numbers with Jakub."

"Yes, and I will. However, I'm sort of in the middle of it right now. I was called in for a cleanup, but the victim's cousins and husband showed up. They want me to discover who hurt the lady. I've worked for one of the cousins before. He's an honorable man."

"Can you extricate yourself from the situation?"

"Yes, but not without Carlos...He's literally surrounded by Poseidon's children." Which was true as they were watching him clean up the shattered vase.

Derrik sighed. "Are you sure you don't love him?"

Even after one hundred and sixty-eight years of being a vampire and all that entailed, Derrik never lost his Victorian ideas about getting married. He was so obsessed with the idea; he wanted me to settle down with anyone—even if he was a decomposing shade and I was stuck in a teenaged body.

"Can we not talk about this right now? Ryan is not answering my text. I really need someone who understands the anatomy of Poseidon's children."

"I believe he is home. We will be there as soon as we can. If not, I'll call you right back."

"We?"

Derrik rarely approved of my existence choices such as owning a condo in Capitol Hill and going to clubs for human blood instead of settling down with one or two enthralled humans, but I could forever rely on his dedication to family.

"I will ensure you don't do anything accidentally illegal or drag your honored brother into illegal activities. Besides, you are not in the position to wait for a car service. Sunrise is at 7:08 AM."

"Thank you, Derrik."

"You can thank me by attending services next Sabbath. I'll have the bedding in your coffin washed. Let us know if Carlos will be attending with you."

It wasn't a request. My heart sank, but I needed help.

"I'll ask him."

I hated missing work on Saturday nights as it was my most profitable night of the week. At least, it was autumn. Historically autumn wasn't as busy as summer. I'd give Carlos PTO whether he came or not, but he liked to keep himself occupied.

Moreover, I wasn't religious. I figured Derrik's God existed—after all, so did vampires—but I doubted They cared if I attended church or not.

I gave a thumbs-up sign to the crowd of people. "Apparently, my lawyer is also coming."

"That didn't sound like a conversation with your

lawyer, more like a conversation with family," Samuel said.

"Was that your dad?" Lilianna asked. "Because it sounded like a dad voice."

"I think the work is creator," Gwenna whispered.

"No. I was created by William, who created by Derrik. Derrik also created Dr. Ryan Jones, who is a marine biologist."

"So Derrik's your grandpa?" Lilianna asked. "And Ryan is your uncle?"

"Yes, but in the coven, we are all equal. Like a witch coven, we tend to use the terms: honored brother, sister, or sibling."

"How old is he?"

"Derrik? Hundred-sixty-nine."

"Years?" Lilianna asked.

"Yes," I said. "Please before my family arrives: Will everyone tell me where you were earlier today?"

"Let's see; I arrived in Seatac at noon." Bianca said, "I took an Uber to Fremont, had some lunch, did some window shopping and went to the grocery store on the corner for supplies. I called Zaria. She said the houseboat would be ready at 5 as we had discussed via email.

"My sisters arrived on the 3 pm."

"You traveled together?"

Gwenna's eyes flickered over to Medea.

"No, I offered to be bumped," Medea said. "I got a free ticket for taking the next plane. So I arrived on the 3:50."

"Always looking for a bargain! Now you two can't alibi each other!" Bianca snapped.

"Who knew we'd need an alibi? Don't be cross,"

Medea said.

I raised my hand. "So you all Ubered to the houseboat?"

"Actually, I took the light rail to the convention center and then took a taxi the rest of the way," Medea said.

"See, always looking for a bargain," Gwenna said.

*Good grief,* I thought. "And is this your first time in Seattle?"

"Not mine," Bianca said.

"And how well do you know the city?" I asked.

"I worked here for a month while I was part of a touring theatre company." She looked down at her wine, but the pride in her work was apparent. "It was so beautiful I wanted to come for a real visit. The front door was open a little when I arrived a little after 5 pm. My sisters arrived a short time after."

"We just dropped off our bags," Medea said. "We were here for maybe fifteen minutes—full of jetlag. We had to get moving. So we left a note."

Gwenna started rambling: "Then we went to MoPop, the Chihuly museum, and Space Needle to see that rotating glass floor."

"When we returned, we found the poor soul on the floor," Bianca sniffed.

"Can you prove that?"

"We have some receipts," Bianca said. "But not all of them—we didn't know we'd need them."

"Of course. Anything to add?"

Medea flexed her hands. "There seems to be many homeless around Seattle. Some are sleeping in the park. They are everywhere. It seems to me that anyone might have hurt the poor woman.

"Maybe someone had followed her into the marina."

"What do you two do for a living?"

"I'm a copywriter," Gwenna said.

"I'm a mail carrier," Medea said.

"How did you ladies choose this place?"

"Zaria's houseboat has a 99% 5-star rating," Bianca said.

"And it was in our budget," Medea said. "The houseboat was quite reasonable split three ways if we held our getaway during the week. And she gave us Sunday on the weekday rate, because of a personal celebration would make coming in on Monday impossible."

"And the pictures were gorgeous," Gwenna said.

"Did you know your hostess was a daughter of Poseidon?"

"How would we have known that?" Medea asked.

"Her profile picture?" I asked.

"It just showed someone who looked like a human—there were some hints that it was welcoming to the supernatural community," Bianca said. "Since she said she was celebrating the new moon, we figured our host was another witch."

"Would you show Carlos the listing?"

Gwenna grabbed her tablet and went to sit beside him. Carlos knew what I was looking for. I wanted to catch them in a lie or discover who the woman in the profile was.

I turned to the children of Poseidon. "Alright, my friends, where were you?"

"We are suspects?" Samuel asked.

"I need to know where everyone was to possibly get a time of death. That might help me solve the crime."

"Today, I went to work. After work, I was playing with my kids." Kellen stretched his back and then looked at the floor.

"And you weren't worried about your wife?" I asked.

"Well, there is all the New Moon Party preparations. I figured she was around," Kellen said. "If I was here....I didn't know she had rented our houseboat. That witch is right. There are so many homeless."

"While, of course, that's a possibility, how would a homeless person get beyond the marina's fence?" I said, hoping they wouldn't try and answer. "Samuel, where were you?"

"Irving and I were at work. We work together at the Kelp factory."

Lilianna wrung her hands. "I don't have a real alibi. I spoke to Zaria earlier in the day—about noon. I was preparing for the New Moon Party: shopping, curing the meats, cleaning. Some of the children saw me. Mine, theirs, and our other kin stopped by for snacks."

"I understand." I nodded. "Now, this might be a tough question, but does Zaria have any enemies?"

"She's just a podwife, who would be her enemy?" Irving said.

"Kellen?"

"What?" He traced his left claw over the serpent on his right shoulder.

"Kellen, sometimes a husband and wife know each other better than anyone. Was there anyone who might have wished her harm?"

"No, she's just a podwife."

"Anyone she's been arguing with?"

"Our eldest daughter wants to get her first personal tattoo, but we told her she has to wait until she's finished with school.

"Really, everyone loved her. Everyone loved her."

I wondered why he said it twice. "Alright, thanks, everyone. I am going to look around."

"Go for it," Gwenna said.

"But I'll be checking my jewelry case before you leave," Bianca said.

Medea was taciturn.

Kellen grumbled under his breath.

"Kellen?" I asked.

"I expect results if you expect us to pay you."

"And if the results are not as you like? As long as I have a solution, you will still pay my bill?"

"It will be paid, Norma," Samuel said. "But we might need to make payments."

"That isn't a problem." I kept my face professional, but I smiled inwardly as I turned away. It's nice to get return business.

# Chapter 4

## 3:30 AM

◆▮◆

**M**Y SILENT FOOTSTEPS PADDED ACROSS the deck. I peeked into a sleeping area set up with three bunk beds, so it slept six. The color scheme was red, white, and blue. How patriotic. None of the beds had been slept in though bags and clothing were sprawled across two of the bottom bunks.

I rarely left Seattle. I could count the times I stayed in a hotel on one hand, but I couldn't stand the idea of my personal belongings being sprawled around in such a manner. Born in the filth of the Victorian era, Derrik would consider it a sign of low-class behavior which he left behind when he became a vampire. Ryan also was fanatical about neatness. Most vampires were.

In my pocket, my phone buzzed: Ryan.

I answered, "Hey."

"Autopsy?" Ryan asked.

"Yeah. Female merfolk found dead in her houseboat, which she uses for short-term rentals. I can give you a thousand dollars."

"A thousand dollars?"

"Is that not fair? I don't really know what the going

rate for an autopsy is." I glanced over my shoulder to make sure that no one was too close.

I heard Derrik say something through the speaker. They must be already walking to the car.

"How do you make money?" Ryan asked, his voice serious.

"I respect people's vices," I said which was true.

"Not funny. I've seen you drop cash during a job. If you're doing something, you shouldn't..."

*Gods, Ryan had no humor, whatsoever.*

"I'm not in trouble. If I solve the crime by dawn, I make 10K. If not, I still get 5K. We are past 2 am, so I probably won't get another job."

"The coven worries."

That was something Derrik wanted to be true. He worried about me, not the coven. Some were pleasant but distant; most pretended I didn't exist. The worst regarded me only as The Shame of the Paper Flower Consortium due to my accidental and too-young rebirth. However, certain vampires of the coven did care. Most of the ancients grew to love me. And Ryan and I had become closer since I exonerated him and his girlfriend, Fern, of staking her ex. Maybe once Fern finished the three-year initiation program and became a vampire too, hopefully, one more vampire would care about me.

"I do what's necessary for the job. Besides, solving crimes are interesting. If you don't want the money, do you know anyone else who can do a merfolk autopsy on such short notice?"

"I'll do it," Ryan said.

"And a grand is fair?"

"Yes, it's fair. More than fair for an unemployed marine biologist."

"Don't say that," I said. "Twice tonight, I've wished for your insight. That's why I texted you. Why didn't you text me back?"

"Oh, sorry, I headed to Derrik's office first to tell him you were in danger and ask him how to proceed. And there you were on the phone with him."

"Why does everyone always assume I'm in danger?" I asked with the hope Ryan didn't answer. "I just need a marine biologist. I'll see you soon."

"See you." Ryan disconnected.

I studied each item carefully but stopped myself from straightening the witches' possessions even though Derrik and Ryan were coming. Obsessiveness was a vampire trait I refused to indulge.

By the size of the clothing, some of the outfits were Gwenna's. The other suitcase belonged to Bianca. Inside, I saw a pink bag filled with cheap jewelry.

That must be what Bianca was referring too. It was gaudy. The metal wasn't even real silver or I would have had an allergic reaction from touching it. I set it aside. Wrapped inside a laundry bag, I found a silver anthame. The ceremonial blade wasn't sharp, but it might kill a vampire in my bloodline if we were stabbed with it. Silver was a common allergy for vampires, but extremely common in bloodlines which dated back to Rome. Hopefully, the witches didn't know that.

I found a small tote bag filled with a few snacks and

magazines, most likely to entertain someone on the flight.

I discovered a nearly empty backpack leaning in the corner filled with a change of casual clothing.

"Where is Medea's bag?" I muttered. Then realized, I should ask since my suspects were talking. I walked back into the living room where Carlos stood like a bouncer between the group of witches who looked as if they were getting more tipsy by the second and the merfolk who looked like they were getting angrier. I wished I could read their minds!

"Medea, where is your suitcase?"

"Oh, I just bring a backpack," she answered too loudly. "I hate checking my bag for twenty-five dollars, sometimes fifty! I figure anything I decide I need I can just buy."

I noticed Medea hadn't answered the question and the answer she gave doesn't really make sense from a budgetary standpoint.

However, I did not have time to get a better answer, because Irving turned from the front window, "Hey what kind of car does your lawyer drive? Because a car just pulled into the parking lot like a barracuda chasing an anchovy."

# Chapter 5

## 3:52 AM

---

I COULDN'T BELIEVE DERRIK HAD GONE over the speed limit. It wasn't like him to break any law. However, he would have had to speed to make it to Fremont from Georgetown that fast. Even this time of night and if he hit all green lights, the coven was at least thirty minutes away. He made it in twenty. I also couldn't believe if Derrik planned to speed he drove his Accord instead of his 1949 Cadillac Series 61 Flashback. I had such good memories of that car. The coven's mechanic kept it in perfect condition and slowly upgraded the systems, so it drove as smooth and fuel efficient as any modern car. Even though Derrik tried to blend in by driving his non-flashy car, but stepping out in his three-piece suit with the long cut jacket pretty much meant he didn't. This was Seattle, after all.

"Who is that?" Lilianna whispered.

"Derrik Miller—my lawyer."

Bianca peeked out the window. "Oh, my God! You didn't tell us your grandpa is such a hottie. I love a man with a well-kept mustache. He has that whole steampunk look."

I didn't know what to say: most of the older vampires had more body and facial hair than modern humans wore,

38

but Derrik always took care of his appearance, especially his immaculately waxed golden mustache. It was part of his identity as a Victorian gentleman. Thanks to hipsters such mustaches were back in style.

He must have just had blood because his alabaster skin looked slightly pink. He could almost pass as human.

"I'm sure Derrik will be pleased to hear that, but he might not know the word hottie."

Ryan slid from the backseat. Crap. That meant someone else was with them.

"And that's your uncle? He's an Adonis," Medea said.

A tall and lean Black man, his features shone not with the blue hue of undeath, but hints of warmth, he, too, must have just fed. His gray wool sweater over his gray shirt gave her the impression he was a professor, at least his pants were still jeans. He held a leather case which no doubt held a set of surgeon's tools.

The witches' faces let me know how much they were enjoying the view. I really wanted them to stop sexualizing my relatives. It made me feel awkwardly protective of them. It also made me jealous of their perfect adult bodies. No one ever enjoyed the view of me unless I spent hours padding my body and doing hair and makeup.

Derrik and Ryan became vampires because the upper-middle-class coven lifestyle suited them. In 1842, Derrik met the elders and spent nine years training to be a vampire under Jakub as he escorted the fledgling coven across the Atlantic, then west across the plains. He learned to read and apprenticed as a lawyer. When he was twenty-seven and a licensed attorney, he was transformed into a vampire.

Ryan came to the coven fresh out of graduate school in the 1980s. He was middle class but tired of not fitting in anywhere. After the standard three-year program, he was initiated into Derrik's bloodline at age 36. Unlike most young vampires, he had not been ashamed to be aligned with Derrik. His scientific curiosity got the better of him. He wanted to know what it was to have the knowledge of people's thoughts.

The coven gave vampires the security of a safe building, loving family and friendships with other vampires and enthralled humans. Outsiders, especially readers of vampire romances, never understood how a too-young body alienated me from the other vampires. (Or perhaps they understood too well.)

Ryan once said he believed that not only my outer shell but my brain and other organs stopped maturing at fourteen, which is why I had an eternal well of energy and couldn't help being headstrong and reckless.

Derrik walked around the car and opened the passenger door. A flash of auburn caught the wind as he held Pascaline's hand.

Carlos nudged me and scribbled in his pad: *Why do I suddenly feel as if I'm at a bring your parents to work day?*

I ran a finger over my eyebrow and took the pen. *Good grief. They think we are in danger.*

Carlos: *We are on a dangerous gig.*

"Oh, my Goddess!" Gwenna squealed. "Is that really Lady Pascaline?"

"Who's that?" Lilianna asked.

"Pascaline Fabron Aubinet Miller, Lady de Bankier," Gwenna said in one breath. "She's a REAL lady. A French noblewoman who escaped the French Revolution and became a vampire."

"Actually, it was the Sun King," I said.

"Whose the Sun King?" Lilianna asked.

"Some old French King long dead, that doesn't matter," Bianca said. "Lady Pascaline and her sister, Lady Loretta, have raised billions of dollars for sick witch children over the past century. But the sisters are so reclusive they never let photographs be taken, only paintings. Even their publicity shots are paintings."

I didn't explain that vampires did not cast a reflection. Photography simply didn't work. Centuries ago, Pascaline became a vampire so she might bring vengeance to the soldiers who killed her family—only she and Loretta survived. Now she and her sister ran charity events, the initiation program. She was coven liaison, but enjoyed the quiet life of vampires.

"I never thought I'd ever get the chance to meet her," Gwenna said. "Oh, my Goddess, you know her?"

"Yeah. She's Derrik's wife," I said. "I used to live with them."

A tiny fib. After Derrik took me in, Pascaline devoted herself to my care and education, but existed in the condo adjacent. Pascaline liked painted French furniture while Derrik's preferred stained wood. They had a happier marriage with separate spaces.

The witches all twittered amongst themselves.

"Why was she gone?" Gwenna asked.

Trying to explain torpor to non-vampires—especially three tipsy witches—was an exercise in futility.

I answered like a vampire: "The great lady had

personal business. You may ask her if you want to know. Do any of you speak French? She speaks English very well but thinks in French. Sometimes she falls into old speech, not realizing."

"I took two years in high school," Medea said.

"Good, I'm sure she'll love to converse in French if you'd like to practice," I said.

"The dirt sheets said, 'before she went away she was seen with a dark-haired vampire with noble bearing'," Gwenna said with a thoughtful expression.

"Yes, her normal escort for fancy parties has dark hair, but he isn't her husband, just her escort," I said, unwilling to explain Pascaline and Laurence's relationship to strangers.

"Norma, do you think this Lady Pascaline would do something for our children?" Lilianna said quietly. "Many are losing scales due to climate change."

"Like all vampires, the lady is concerned about climate change. The specifics might be a bit messy since she's not able to breathe underwater, but she might be able to organize a benefit or something. You should speak to her while I'm trying to solve the case."

"She'd really help us?" Lilianna said with a bit of hope in her voice.

"Just talk to her," I insisted.

In a loose flowing black gown, Pascaline seemed to float as she walked. Her auburn curls offset her freckled alabaster skin, but she too was touched with pink. At over three hundred years old, Pascaline didn't blink or move enough to pass as human, and she was beyond caring.

Not that it mattered to the witches. The witches all

curtsied to Pascaline. They were so excited to surround her and touch her icy hands.

"May we get a selfie, Lady Pascaline?" Bianca asked. "Our fellow covens are going to be so jealous!"

"I would love to, dear, but only my gown would show up. I didn't think to put on cosmetics." She gently pressed them to back up so the men could enter the small houseboat. "This is my husband, Derrik Miller, and my husband's Second Born, Dr. Ryan Jones."

"Why did you come?" Bianca asked.

"Certainly, dears, you must be aware Norma called for our help."

Bianca clarified, "Yes, but why did you, Lady Pascaline, come?"

"I've been so excited to see Norma at work. She solved a murder as I was away on personal business. Derrik, of course, is always concerned she might find danger, but *ma petite crevette* has a good head on her shoulders. Our family is delighted to have Mr. Fisher-Perez with us. A true friend is the greatest of treasures."

Carlos inclined his head at her.

"Ma petite what?" Gwenna gushed.

"It's just an endearment," I said.

"What does it mean?"

"Translated it means my little shrimp," I said, already annoyed at my family.

The mermen started laughing. Samuel elbowed me gently. "Little shrimp?"

"So they are like your parents."

The witches were squealing and twittering again.

They refilled their glasses of wine and pulled out another glass for Pascaline. "Does anyone else want anything?" Gwenna called. "It looks like we'll be here for awhile."

"There should be some clam jam and sardines in the fridge," Lilianna said. "I'll make up some snacks."

"I'll help." Irving reached into the fridge.

Gwenna was kind enough to get Lilianna a wine glass and coffee mugs for the men.

I pressed down my annoyance. Pascaline might appear as the gentle French noblewoman, but she was an exceptionally physically strong and fast vampire. Derrik was just as gifted of a mind reader as me, not that it was doing any good on this night. Plus he knew the legalities of most of my work which kept me on the right side of the law. It was good that they came.

Gwenna touched Ryan's chest. "I don't suppose you've ever had witch blood before."

He stepped back and put his surgery case in front of him. "No, Madam, I have not. Also, I have a lover—a vampire initiate—in the program.

"Norma, if you please, show me the daughter of Poseidon."

*Can you hear me? I can't read their minds,* Derrik thought to Ryan and I. Pascaline did not have the gift to speak without speaking, but she was close enough to Derrik to at least hear echoes of the conversation.

*I think they cast some type of shielding spell before Carlos and I arrived,* I replied in the same way.

*I can sense some thoughts from Poseidon's Children, or at least their emotions.* Ryan thought. *But nothing from the witches.*

*Same.* I said.

*No wonder this puzzle has captured you?* Derrik smiled, showing a glint of fang. *I admit, it has captured me too. Why would someone cast a shielding spell?*

I thought back, *Just a guess: because they don't know our gifts, but know the legends. Bianca, maybe all the witches, seems to have watched a lot of vampire movies.*

"So you all live in a coven? How exciting!" Bianca said, her eyes shifting between Derrik and Pascaline's faces.

"We live there due to the lack of excitement," Pascaline answered her.

"I bet you have great orgies. Perhaps..."

Derrik blushed. "Please, my progenies..." He gestured towards Ryan and me.

The children of Poseidon looked just as embarrassed.

"I think, dear ladies, the orgy days were over, long before the second and third-generation vampires were reborn," Ryan said.

"Still, I would love to see a vampire coven on a Sabbath," Bianca said dreamily.

"Everyone is welcome to the Sabbath," Pascaline said.

"There's even a potluck after services," I added.

The idea of returning to the coven life made me want to rip out someone's throat. I considered if Bianca was the murderer, maybe I would get the chance.

"What if I wanted to give my blood to someone?" Bianca asked.

I wouldn't rip out Bianca's throat after all. I hunted the evil, not the stupid.

Derrik and Ryan were blushing now.

"You would need to know who you wanted to give it too..." Pascaline started to say. "The coven has many vampires. Some of them are in monogamous relationships, but not all are."

"You just don't take it?" She looked positively disappointed.

"Only if you ask for your special someone to take it first. And they know your limits. Norma, what is the modern parlance again?"

"Safeword," I said, pressing my fingers to my temples.

"Yes, safeword," Pascaline said. "You need to ensure your vampire knows your safeword."

"Can you please let me see the body?" Ryan begged.

"This way."

I also wanted to get back to work. If I was going to solve the mystery before dawn in front of the closest thing I had to vampire parents and my better-looking, perfect coven brother, I needed to keep my mind on the puzzle.

# Chapter 6

## 4:00 AM

R YAN TOOK OFF HIS SWEATER AND ROLLED up his sleeves. I gave him one of Carlos's coveralls to protect his clothing, and helped him step into them. Ryan was six inches taller than Carlos, but not nearly as muscular; he swam in the garment. At least, Carlos's large-sized latex gloves fit his hands.

I cleared the breakfast bar. Carlos lifted Zaria's body and gently placed her upon it.

However, as well-mannered as any vampire, Ryan inclined his head and then carefully met eyes with each of the four Children of Poseidon. "I am not a pathologist, and as a land dweller, I have limited experience with merfolk anatomy, but I will be respectful to your beloved wife and kinswoman's remains." While those words were true, he had also done several merfolk autopsies during his last study.

I set up my recorder to take his notes.

Samuel snaked over to him. "I would like to watch this autopsy in order my kinswoman's body is not despoiled in any way."

"You may watch, but many find an autopsy of their own kind gruesome. I will be respectful and whenever possible

follow the lines along with the injury so she is damaged as little as possible," Ryan said. "See this row of scales? I can cut underneath that to open the chest cavity with minimal visual scarring."

"Thank you, Dr. Jones."

"If it pleases you, you may call me Ryan. My honored sister and Carlos go by their given names."

"Then please call me Sam."

"I wish her husband was as apprehensive as you are, Sammy," Irving muttered.

"Perhaps, he is overwrought," I suggested. "People sometimes don't know what to do in stressful situations and seem uncaring, but they are, in reality, frozen by all their emotions swirling around."

Bianca's lips parted.

I knew what she was going to say before she said it.

"Perhaps, Kellen doesn't want to be in the room, because your kinswoman did not have the happiest of marriages, Samuel."

Samuel's eyes pinched into blue lines. "What would you know about that, witch?"

Studying them, I wondered that myself.

"It is obvious."

"Please, people, let me work. We don't have much time," Ryan said.

Ryan examined Zaria's head for injury. He found a large bump on the back of her head hidden by her thick and glossy scales. He gently prodded her arms and tail, testing for rigor.

"Can you give me a time of death?" I asked.

"Well I can't give you an exact time, but sometime this afternoon. I'd say before 3 PM, but that's as good as I can give you. With their lower body temperature, merfolk go into rigor much slower than most land creatures when they die in a cool environment."

"The only person who doesn't have an alibi for that time is Lilianna," Samuel said. "But if you saw the spread, she set out for the party; you would know it couldn't be her. There was too much work to be done."

"Ladies, was the air-conditioning on when you arrived?" I asked.

"I don't know," Bianca said.

Medea added, "You know it was a little chilly. Gwenna grabbed a shawl, and then we stepped outside and realized it was a perfect sixty-five degrees."

Ryan sliced into the damaged torso using a modified Y incision, careful to respect the merfolk's traditions.

He called, "Norma, if you please." His voice was cool, but I heard the undertone of panic.

"This is wrong," he whispered.

"What do you mean?"

"Someone has already cut open Zaria's body."

"But why?"

"The only reason I can think of..." He paused and turned his scalpel sideways, he slid open the Y incision. "The skin was held together by glue."

"Glue?"

"Many glues have been used to hold flesh together," Ryan said. As soon as he opened her chest, even I could see Zaria's heart was missing.

"By the God of Blood, could there be a poacher in Seattle?" Ryan said.

"Have you heard of any?" I asked the merfolk.

Samuel gasped. "But we haven't seen such people for a century!"

"Irving, could you ask her husband for permission to continue the examination? I apologize, but I must open her throat."

"You believe it's a poacher then?" Samuel asked.

"The bump on the head, the missing heart...if the double larynx is missing who else could it be?" Ryan asked. "I shall observe the rest of the organs.

A thought slipped into my brain. I wasn't sure if it was Ryan's or my own, but I bit my tongue before it slipped out. *It might have been someone who wanted us to believe it was a poacher.*

*Indeed.* Ryan thought back.

Samuel returned, wobbling. Leaning on the cased opening, he said, "Kellen says do whatever you need to do. He is less concerned about the state of the body."

"Now this is strange. She had salmon for lunch."

"We eat fish..."

"Yes, I know, but she had cooked salmon, sliced into a fillet with what looks like orange slices and baby potatoes and kale."

While Ryan checked the rest of the organs, I found the garbage bin in the kitchen. *What did the witches eat?*

This garbage held a few inner seals for food items and one for juice.

Ryan sewed the incision so carefully and delicately

that Zaria's scales covered it. Then he opened her throat following the lines of her fine scales. As he suspected, her double larynx has been removed.

*If someone wanted us to believe it was a poacher, would they have thrown these organs away?* I asked Ryan with my mind. *Because if the organs are in the lake, there's no way we're going to find them.*

Ryan thought back to me: *Maybe the heart, but a mermaid's double larynx is so valuable no one would just throw it away.*

"Okay so my next step is to check the dumpster in front of the marina," I said.

"You dumpster dive?" Derrik asked.

"Carlos and I do whatever needs to be done. We have online reviews to think of," I said.

"Must you make a joke about everything? I have a dead body here," Ryan said.

Samuel cleared his throat. "Don't worry, Ryan.

"Zaria would've liked Norma's sense of humor. In fact, I think she might have liked seeing a vampire family. I'm sorry she missed it."

C ARLOS BROUGHT ME THE AD ON THE IPAD and his notebook. Zaria's pictures were gorgeous, yet obviously not taken by a professional. There were too many weird angles and shadows.

Carlos: **Her profile picture is just a royalty-free image. She didn't let people know she was a merwoman until they got here.**

"So another reason it probably wasn't a poacher, unless someone staked out the houseboat. Ryan has discovered the larynx and heart is missing."

**Carlos: Previous guest, maybe?**

"Hmm, good point," I said as I scanned the ad.

*LAKE UNION HOUSEBOAT FOR RENT $400 A NIGHT*

*LISTEN TO THE SEA LIONS SING AS YOU ENJOY THIS CHARMING 1920'S VINTAGE HOUSEBOAT WITH HOTEL-LIKE AMENITIES. GREAT FOR ROMANTIC WEEKENDS, GIRLS' WEEKEND, OR BACHELORETTE PARTIES!*

*WALKING DISTANCE FROM FREMONT SHOPPING AND GAS WORKS PARK. ON THE EXPRESS BUS LINE TO DOWNTOWN. MASTER SUITE WITH PILLOW TOP KING SIZED BED AND BUNK ROOM WHICH SLEEPS SIX. BLACKOUT DRAPES ON ALL THE WINDOWS. LIVING ROOM WITH A WIDESCREEN TELEVISION, PS4, DVD, AND BOARD GAME LIBRARY. ROWBOAT AND FISHING EQUIPMENT FOR RENT WITH ADVANCE NOTICE.*

*TWO-NIGHT MINIMUM WEEK DAY RATES: CALL FOR INFO! FREE JAR OF HOME-MADE CLAM JAM WITH EVERY STAY! GREAT WITH FRESH SALMON OR CRACKERS! VERY WELCOMING TO SPECIAL NEEDS GUESTS!*

Carlos: **You know how she mentions clam jam and special needs guests. That might hint that she was part of** the community. Gwenna said the line about special needs guests was why they chose this place.

I whispered: "Though Medea mentioned her budget, this is not a budget place. $400 a night."

Carlos: Yeah. No kidding. But check out the reviews, This has been a haven for the supernatural community for some time.

I scrolled down.

*"ZARIA'S THE BEST HOST. CLAM JAM SOUNDS WEIRD, BUT IT IS DELICIOUS! WE ARE A SPECIAL NEEDS FAMILY WITH UNCOMMON RELIGIOUS REQUIREMENTS AND ZARIA HELPED WITH ALL OF THEM!"*

*"ZARIA IS SUCH A TREAT. SHE'S A BIT ZANY, BUT THEN SEATTLE IS THE ZANIEST MAJOR CITY I'VE EVER BEEN. SHE KNEW ALL ABOUT PLACES WHERE SPECIAL NEEDS FOLK WOULD BE WELCOME. HER CLAM JAM IS FANTASTIC. I BOUGHT SIX EXTRA JARS TO TAKE HOME."*

The reviews went on. Carlos was right.

I kept whispering: "Ryan said no one would have thrown siren organs away because they are so valuable, but I figure we have to be sure."

Carlos: Time for a dumpster dive?

I nodded. "Unless you want me to do it."

Carlos: Damn! I had to know I wouldn't get to sit with three sexy and drunk witches all night.

"So Zaria had cooked salmon and potatoes for lunch. Maybe some airline tickets and receipts, something that proves the witch's story," I said.

Carlos: No prob.

"I'm going upstairs. I still haven't seen Medea's real bag. Only a backpack too light even for a weekend unless she doesn't change her underwear."

Carlos: **Maybe she doesn't wear them. Some hippy-chicks don't.**

I nodded and pressed my lips together to hold back giggling. As far as I knew that might be a clue and if I was planning on investigating murders, Carlos and I needed to be able to speak of every clue. "Good point."

We fist-bumped and went to our respective tasks.

# Chapter 7

## 4:15 AM

———◆❧◆———

WHILE RYAN FOCUSED ON HIS AUTOPSY, and Carlos searched through the trash, I slowly moved through the small houseboat. It seemed extra small with all the people in the main room. *Observe. There must be clues about what happened to Zaria.*

I climbed the spiral staircase to the second deck. A large bed dominated this level. Two upholstered armchairs sat next to the sliding door which led outside to a patio, overlooking the lake and with views of downtown.

The blankets on the bed were slightly lopsided, but I couldn't tell if it was some style or not. I lifted the bedding. The bed was a storage type with drawers. I opened each one. I found more blankets, raincoats, umbrellas, and winter clothing. Nothing out of the ordinary there.

The reviews were right. This was a lovely rental. Beside one of the chairs, I found another backpack. The women's clothes stuffed inside were more casual.

*Could this be Medea's bag? But why would it up here if they were dropping things off?*

I searched through the backpack. Medea traveled very light for a trip to Seattle. Unless she had unpacked and put her things in the closet, Carlos was right about the underwear.

I checked the closet.

It was empty, except hangers, an ironing board, and iron.

I N THE BEDSIDE DRAWER, I FOUND AN OPEN box of Night of Titan mermaid shaped condoms and a box of standard condoms. (Mermaid shaped condoms covered the merman's genital flaps for complete protection since a merman's penis was normally hidden from view like other marine mammals.) Several were missing, but that didn't mean anything. A mermaid owned this property.

"Norma, what are you doing?" Pascaline asked.

"Looking for clues."

"Why?"

"Because Poseidon's Children won't let the witches go without proof of their innocence."

"And how does that affect us?" Pascaline said.

"Quality customer service protects all of us, as does my street cred. Ask Derrik if you don't believe me."

"You were supposed to get rid of the body, oui?"

"Yes."

"But you can't do that."

"After the autopsy, I will repack for transport. The children of Poseidon will bury her as their custom."

"There is only two and a half hours or so before till dawn, *ma crevette*. While you are healthy now, you've been injured more than any other vampire due to your work."

"We are immortal, I'm going to get hurt sometimes," I said, this time not making a joke.

"Needlessly hurt."

"I doubt Ryan and Fern would say that catching a killer was needless."

"But without a thrall, how will you get blood?" Pascaline asked.

"I will find an evil human and kill for it. I appreciate your concerns, Callie," I said using Pascaline's nickname that only Loretta and I used to soften the message. "I help people. This is what I do."

I noticed an open merman-style condom wrapper under one of the chairs. Snapping a pair of gloves on her hands, I gathered it and put it in a zipper-baggy.

"You weren't nearly this stubborn when you were young. Derrik and I worry about you," she said.

"I know. Ryan already reminded me."

"Derrik shouldn't have to make deals to get you to attend services," Pascaline said.

"You know how I feel about God."

"And you know how we feel about Him. Our feelings are irrelevant. You are a member of the coven and the more we flaunt rules, the more we must do what is expected."

"You don't flaunt rules."

"I've lived centuries longer than you," Pascaline said. "And I hurt Agata and Jakub and Loretta and all who love me before I learned to behave as a vampire."

There was a childish part of me that wanted to point out her mistakes, but the adult side won out.

"Callie, please listen to me. The neighbors already

threatened to call the police. If the police are called, they will see there are merfolk and witches. It would be everywhere. The merfolk's underwater cities would be rushed. I don't know what might happen to the witches, but I don't want to return to the days of religious persecution. Enough people are getting attacked due to their race or gender in the news already."

"Yes, but most of those are humans. After Ryan finishes the autopsy, come home with us."

"I can't. I don't belong there."

I opened the sliding glass door and scanned the patio, but other than a few stray leaves in the corners, it was clear other than the plastic deck chairs and table.

"You are a vampire." Pascaline started speaking in French, a few older pronunciations, but I understood easily enough. I had heard this before. Roughly translated, Pascaline said, "You belong with us. Find a job in the coven and stop this insane nonsense for Derrik's sake. Never was any progeny loved as you are."

Trying to get Pascaline to help or at least stop talking in French, I snapped, "Look, if you really want to help, go talk to Poseidon's children about organizing a charity event for them."

"I already gave them my information. I will help them any way I can. All those poor little babies—their infant mortality rate is so high." Her eyes brimmed with bloody tears. She took out a handkerchief and dabbed gently. Before she became a vampire, she had lost her only child due to a chill when they escaped from the soldiers who were hell-bent on raping and murdering them.

"I'm sorry, Callie. I didn't mean to hurt you."

"A mother's love for her child is as immortal as she is," Pascaline said.

I didn't see a wastebasket in the bedroom, so I went into the en-suite to check under the sink. Bottles of sunscreen, insect repellent, and allergy medicine stood on the counter. Below was mostly empty except a bit of tissue and a used condom. Gross, but expected. No hostess with a 5-star rating would have left that in the bathroom. I checked the shower. The bar of soap was damp as was the shower floor.

Derrik called up the stairs. "Ryan wants to see you."

I went downstairs.

Ryan's paced the kitchen. "Zaria did not die from the bump on the head. She died via suffocation. There is damage all over her gills. A poacher would not have killed her this way."

"So those were my thoughts earlier?" I worked so hard on my mind-reading skills, not to have them left me lost.

"Honestly, I don't know. We were sort of thinking the same thoughts," Ryan said.

I came closer. "How strong would a person have to be to suffocate a merwoman?"

"Strong enough to incapacitate them. Or they would need to be close to her."

"I never really stayed at any short-term rentals before. If you were a landlady, would you let your guests that close?" I asked.

"Probably not, but if it were the witches, it'd have to be all three of them. Maybe two."

I pressed my lips together. I needed to get Bianca

alone. If she was the first one here, she might know who all had been in the houseboat.

"Bianca, would you come upstairs with me, please?" I asked.

Bianca was not happy about being pulled away from the others, though she did like holding Pascaline's arm in that gentle way noblewomen used to do.

"Oh, *ma chérie*, it's nothing really to worry about, Norma just had a question for you."

"You said you were here first?" I asked.

"Yes," Bianca said, in a sarcastic tone.

"Did you have intimate relations with a son of Poseidon?"

"No! How dare you ask me that! This is the worse vacation ever." Tears ran down her cheeks.

"*Ma chérie, ne pleure pas!*" Pascaline pulled out a lace handkerchief and dabbed her cheeks.

"What?" Bianca asked through her tears. Pascaline handed her the small lace square.

Pretending the earlier conversation about bloodletting and sexualizing my realitives had not happened, I said, "She told you not to cry. Vampires talk of sex openly, we sometimes forget others don't. I'm sorry I upset you."

Carlos texted. I found a bag that is from the houseboat. Lunch and its wrappers: Salmon, potatoes, some bakery box for dessert. No airline tickets or receipts from today. Or anything that looks like an organ.

I texted back: Cool, thanks, come in.

"Bianca, what did you eat for lunch?"

"What? Oh, I had a salad with chicken on it. You

might not understand, but it's hard to keep your figure after forty," Bianca said sadly.

"Did you eat that here?"

"No, some little café in Fremont—then I went to the store for wine and cheese and other goodies."

I couldn't read her mind, but my instincts were telling me that Bianca was telling the truth. Even for her earlier words, she wasn't a party girl. She was a person who was upset and getting more upset by the minute.

"I'm sorry for Zaria Poseidondottier, but my sisters and I didn't hurt her."

Pascaline patted Bianca's hand. "Norma is trying to help."

"With all your errands, you're sure you were the first of your sisters to arrive?" I asked.

"I don't see how they could have gotten here first, especially with Seattle's afternoon traffic," Bianca said.

I understood. Even on Sundays, the commute into the city from the south on I-5 could mean traffic—especially on Game Days or other special events.

# Chapter 8

## 4:46 AM

I ESCORTED THE WOMEN AS WE RETURNED downstairs. Bianca held the lace handkerchief with a tight fist. I figured Pascaline would never get that back now. Not that my honored sister would care; vampires bought those things by the dozen.

"What did they want?" Gwenna asked her sister.

"They wanted to know if I had sex with anyone," Bianca said with a sniff.

"The reason I asked that is, Lilianna, would you say that Zaria cleaned the houseboat before every guest?" I asked.

"Of course."

I held up the baggie. "Because I just found this under the bed and the garbage holds the used condom which I won't be taking out."

"Thank God," Derrik muttered. "Solving crimes is disgusting."

"It's in the merman style," I said. Inside, my nerves were buzzing, but I ensured my expression was all business.

The three witches start screaming about being ill-used, slut-shamed by vampires, and framed by the merfolk.

"I am not slut-shaming. I don't care who had sex.

I'm trying to figure out everything that happened in this houseboat today," I said. "Who was where and when."

Derrik buried his face in his hands. "If it were only the era of Victoria, I could take up smoking again. Or I could have tried cocaine. Then I wouldn't care about my progeny's manners."

For some reason, that comment made people curious and quiet.

"Why don't you smoke?" Gwenna asked. "It's not like you are going to die."

"Because my wife doesn't like the smell in her curtains and our current generation of humans also tend to despise it. Second-hand smoke causing cancer and all," Derrik said. "Vaping isn't the same."

Trying to keep the conversation on track, I asked, "Did anyone hook up in the houseboat today?"

No one said anything.

"Is it possible Zaria...?"

Kellen looked at his tail, which he stretched out in front of him.

"How dare you speak ill of the dead?" Irving screamed. "In front of her husband no less. How dare you?"

I thought he was a little too enraged by the thought of his cousin having an affair - especially when Kellen seemed so suddenly withdrawn. "Because I have three hours to solve a mystery," I said. "I am going back upstairs—something is tickling my brain."

"Even if Zaria did have an affair, I wouldn't have killed her for it. Payback's a shark as they say," Kellen said softly.

"Couldn't you take Carlos?" Derrik asked.

"He's still outside, I think," I said.

"Then I'm coming with you."

"Can I go to the bunk room?" Bianca asked. "I think I might lie down."

"Sure," I said.

Once we were upstairs, Derrik whispered, "You must work harder not to upset people. Everyone is under so much stress."

"There was very little blood spilled on the floor, but I should've taken more pictures," I said to Derrik. "I still don't know anything about blood splatter—except from my work."

"I don't know, my lamb, it seems like you are causing yourself much grief. Your job is dangerous enough."

"But vampires aren't really hunting anymore. My business needs to offer more services if I am to survive."

"Come home. Go back to university."

I wasn't sure if Derrik meant buying a condo in the Paper Flower Consortium or I should come live in my old coffin-room at his place.

"It's fun to visit, but I like my life in the city proper."

I pushed back the covers on the bed. I unrolled a long strip of tape and pressed it against the sheets. Scales sparkled stuck to the tape.

"I never stopped you from going to clubs even when you lived at home," Derrik said.

Then I knew.

"How would Hugo feel about me moving back in?"

Hugo was Derrik's current thrall, but their relationship was more like an old married couple who dressed exceptionally well. Derrik treated all his human companions as if they were partners and put their happiness first.

"Hugo loves you; Maria loves you too. She never had grandchildren. You would be a great comfort to her if you visited more."

Maria was Hugo's mother. Derrik lost his mother when he was ten-years-old. After she retired, Derrik purchased a studio apartment down the hall from them so she might be close in her dotage.

"Fine. I told you I'd go Saturday, why do you care about this so much?" I felt a flood of emotion for the first time since they arrived. His pain hurt me, but I would not cry for him. Not on the job.

"Because, my sweet lamb, I want you to consider turning Fern," Derrik said.

My mouth opened wide. That was not what I was expecting.

I weighed only ninety-eight pounds. Since 1921, the initiation rites suggested vampires under one hundred and fifteen pounds should not reproduce due to the high chance of the recruit or vampire losing too much blood. The vampire would go into torpor, but the recruit would die. Historically, their greater body weight was one of the reasons more male or male-presenting vampires survived the rite than cis females.

"It is a rather simple ratio. Fern only weighs a hundred and three pounds. There is a greater size difference between me and Ryan than you and Fern."

"So you and Ryan aren't going to fatten her up?"

"We've tried, but she's too concerned about her figure," Derrik said. "If you think I'm wrong..."

"I don't know what to think if I'm honest. For nearly

seventy years, the vampires have told me I shouldn't turn someone due to my size. But I trust you so if Fern's willing, we should at least talk about it with her about it."

"She's worried about being the Shame's daughter."

"Of course, she is," I said flatly. "I'm worried about accidentally killing Ryan's beloved. He would never forgive me."

"But your powers are growing, and you've not had an offspring. If it worked, the offspring would be a powerful vampire," Derrik said. "The unfortunate events at the coven showed me how much this bloodline must expand."

Only Derrik would call one murder, one manslaughter, one staking of a vampire (who recovered!), and execution of another vampire "unfortunate events".

That was just his way.

He went on: "And I don't, and have never, considered you to be the Shame of the Paper Flower Consortium. However, I have allowed others to believe and say what they will for too long."

I smiled. "I will speak to Fern and Ryan on Saturday if you think she will accept me as her creator and mentor." Turning away from him, I said, "Some merfolk had sex since the last time these sheets were laundered."

"Good grief, my lamb." Derrik blushed.

"You're right. They might have just slept here," I said. "But under the covers."

"Have you ever had a son of Poseidon?" Samuel asked from the door. He was not talking to me.

Derrik's blush grew deeper.

Embarrassed as I felt, I shrugged and tried to push

information towards my ancestor. *Samuel's a former client, but I don't know much about him except that he worked in the Kelp factory and loves to sing too close to shore.*

"By the blood," Derrik said. "I had no idea solving murders was so exciting. Was that really an offer, Sir?"

"Well, our people can't grow hair...and you have some on your face. Plus Norma said you are over a century. You must've picked up a few things."

"I'm a married man."

"Yeah, but your wife already told us vampires aren't monogamous due to your long lifespans."

That wasn't true. Some vampires, like Pascaline's sister, Loretta and her husband, had a monogamous relationship that spanned centuries. However, Derrik and Pascaline had a polygamous relationship.

"Hey," I said. "If you're going to do stuff, can you please go outside?"

"Why?" Samuel asked.

"Uh, because I'm still looking for clues in here. There's both kinds of condoms in the nightstand." *If you go outside, can you see if you can read his mind?* I asked Derrik.

*Norma, I am not going outside. I'm here to protect you. If Samuel wants to make love, we can do it another time.* Derrik paused. *Assuming he's not the killer.*

*I don't think so, but I haven't ruled him out. I haven't ruled anyone out.* I raised an eyebrow. *What were you doing today?*

*I was in my coffin—like a normal vampire.* Aloud, Derrik said, "I appreciate the offer, and I admit I'm interested in the experience, but I don't really know you...and..."

"I might have killed my cousin? I didn't."

"But you seem to be in good spirits?" I asked Samuel.

Samuel's eyes opened wider. "Well, as good as anyone can be who had a death in the family, but mostly you, Carlos, and Ryan are trying to solve a murder—I'm just here and so is your grandpa."

"Do you think Zaria would have had an affair?" I asked. "Because between the condom and the scales on the bed, someone used this room for some lovemaking."

"No, not an affair," Samuel said.

"Would she have left Kellen?"

He nodded slowly. "Yes. I believe she would if she could."

"And how would he have responded? Back downstairs, he said he wouldn't have killed her. Do you believe him?"

"He wouldn't have killed her. He might have broken some stuff. Yelled definitely."

"Have you seen him abuse her?" Derrik asked. His loathing of people who abused others was seen clearly on his face. He, especially, loathed men who abused their smaller and weaker partners and/or their children.

Samuel looked away. "Not seen, no."

"Does he hit the kids?" Derrik asked, showing his fangs.

"No, he loves his kids," Samuel wisely said.

Derrik and Pascaline were both protective of children. Derrik would have tried to tear Kellen to pieces. Pascaline would have finished the job. And I'd have another murder to clean up.

"But?" I prodded.

"Well, Zaria has had bruises around her throat. And every year she grew quieter—less herself. Kellen says it was because she's a mother and the children become more central to her life."

"What did Zaria say?" Derrik asked.

"Nothing. She sang with the family. She spoke of her children. I didn't even know she owned a short-term rental," Samuel said. "I should have known, it was her mother's before her."

"Now, that we are alone, besides Kellen, did Zaria ever have problems with anyone? Anyone at all?" I asked.

Samuel scratched his arm at the crease where the fin met the scales. "Well, Irving wanted her recipe for clam-pepper jam, but that's hardly a reason to kill someone. It was a fun feud. She'd make it. He'd try to copy it. They'd joke around about special ingredients. Try new things. You get the idea."

"Irving likes to cook?" I asked.

"Yes. Or at least grill on hot rocks in the summer. Have you ever had salmon with clam jam? It's the best," Samuel said.

# Chapter 9

## 5:00 AM

RETURNING DOWNSTAIRS, I FIGURED I must have gotten ten thousand steps just going up and down stairs of this houseboat.

Carlos stood beside Ryan as he sewed up Zaria's body. I appreciated Carlos would always protect the vampires of my bloodline (and Pascaline) without instruction, so no one needed to feel weird about it.

Kellen said softly, "You did a good job, Dr. Jones. I can barely see the cuts. She looks like she's just sleeping."

"Thank you, sir, I wish we could have met under better circumstances." Ryan took a deep breath, removed the bloody gloves.

He carefully removed the coveralls, not to get any mermaid blood on his clothing. Then handed it to me who put it in a garbage bag.

He turned to wash his hands.

"Careful. The sink backs up," Gwenna said to Ryan.

I perked my ears at that. "Carlos, I will rewrap Zaria's remains for transport. Would you mind helping them unclog the sink? You know how many things collect in the u-bend. Or the garbage disposal."

With a knowing smile, Carlos hurried out to the van for our toolkit.

"Have any of you tried to use the garbage disposal tonight?" I asked.

"No," Bianca said from the couch.

"I can't deal with this anymore," Irving said, moving toward the door.

"You're not leaving." Kellen stood in front of him. "None of us are leaving till we learn which witch did this and we drown her."

"I just meant I want to go upstairs and collect my thoughts," Irving said. I heard the lie in his tone. He wanted out, but he did not dare say so to Kellen. "My kinswoman was just autopsied! I shouldn't have watched that. I might never sleep again."

Carlos removed the flange and pulled out chunks of flesh, mixed with some other brown goo.

Ryan squished his brow together. "I can't say for sure." He sniffed it. "I smell fish, clams. The pink flesh looks kind of like salmon, but I don't want to be wrong. It's not a mermaid's heart."

"Thank Poseidon," Kellen muttered and made the sign of the fish across his chest.

Taking every care to move the woman gently, I wrapped Zaria's corpse for transport. I cleaned up the bloody gore and leakage from the autopsy. Carlos reinstalled the garbage disposal.

After he washed his hands, he texted Derrik.

"The sink is fixed," Derrik announced to the others in the living room.

"Your granddaughter really does believe in customer service. Her quality of work is exceptional. Look at this table, she did earlier, you can barely see the scratch," Gwenna said. "You must be very proud of her."

"I am proud of both of my descendants."

Once the kitchen was spotless again, most of the others had moved into the living room or upstairs.

I quickly glanced through the cupboards. Most of it seemed pretty normal: dishes, pans, knives for preparing food, cutlery. One cabinet was filled with shipping supplies and labels that read: "Bring a taste of Zaria's Houseboat home with you!"

The fridge was filled with wine, a cheese platter, grapes, and fancy cupcakes from the bakery in Fremont. Perfect goodies for a girls' trip.

In the freezer, there was jars and jars of clam jam carefully lined up and dated. There was also frozen fish. Most were small jars, but behind them were a few larger jars dated and labeled for parties — one for that very day.

I noticed the cabinet in the kitchen should be deeper. I found a stepstool and pointed this out to Carlos.

I opened the upper cabinet. There were a few vases and extra mugs and plates: a full set. "Why would there be two sets of dishware in a guest house?"

I knocked on it. "It has a false back."

I passed the dishes down to Carlos who set it on the breakfast bar. I moved a wooden panel.

Behind the panel was a combination safe.

"Kellen, would you come into the kitchen please?" I called.

He glided into the kitchen with a frown.

"Do you know what your wife keeps in this safe?" I asked.

"No. Our documents are kept in our home."

"Do you know the code?"

"No."

"What's your eldest's birthdate?"

"May 12, 2004."

Carlos typed 5-1-2-0-4 into the keypad. It opened.

Inside was a ledger and a large stack of American hundred-dollar bills.

"Wow," I said. "Did you know your wife kept money in this wall safe?"

"Money?" Samuel came in to see what excitement was about.

Kellen grabbed Samuel's arm as he looked inside. The men's eyes bulged, and their mouths widened into smiles at the sight of the money, but Lilianna didn't seem surprised at all. She turned around and went upstairs. I guessed she knew about her friend's emergency stash.

"Of course. I didn't realize it was this much, but yes, of course, I knew about the safe." He fidgeted with his cellphone which he hid in his spine belt. "But this amount of money...she just rented the houseboat as something to do because all our kids have started school. She didn't make a ton of money."

"Are you your wife's beneficiary?"

"In our culture, it is more likely something to go straight to the children, but I would manage it until they were of age."

*Norma, I've seen this before.* Derrik thought. *This woman was siphoning money out of her household. Women do this because they want a divorce or because their husbands are gamblers. We already know he abused her. Just get him to admit his guilt and let's go home.*

Ever since I solved the mystery of who staked a vampire of my coven, I had been watching lots of cop shows. Many times, the police looked to the husband first.

Even without my mindreading abilities, it was apparent Kellen didn't want to be in the houseboat. He might co-own the property with his wife, but he was a stranger in this place.

"How often do you come to this houseboat?"

He looked up to the left. "I was here when my wife received it."

"How did she pay for it?"

"She got it as an inheritance once her mother died. I wanted her to sell it, but she wanted to fix it up and use it as a rental just like her mom," Kellen said. "I should have been more supportive."

I had seen many personalities, both public and private, in eighty-three years. I had seen his type: outwardly gruff, taciturn, unloving to everyone but his kids. He cared about traditions more than their purpose.

"How old are your children?" I asked.

*How is this interrogation?* Derrik asked in my brain, barely hiding his fury at a wife abuser. I didn't react, but Ryan cringed. All the vampires wanted Kellen to be guilty. If the merfolk would let him, Derrik would rip out Kellen's throat right now.

Kellen slapped the beam as he snapped, "Why does that matter?"

"Please, I'm trying to exonerate witnesses here."

"My eldest is sixteen; the triplets are fifteen. Then I have another set of triplets who are ten, and my youngest twins are four," Kellen grumbled.

"Would Zaria ever willingly leave her children behind?" I asked.

Kellen punched a wall, nearer to me than was wise.

I didn't bother ducking, but Carlos and Derrik stepped between us. The low guttural growl rumbled in Carlos's chest. He had no love for men who beat women either. (Or people who beat people.)

"You might want to move away from my progeny before you punch any walls," Derrik said.

"Look, my marriage wasn't all ale and clams, but no marriage is," Kellen said as he slid backward. He squirmed away grumbling about how he should fill the pontoons with water and drown everyone.

Carlos texted: **Be careful. That guy is under a lot of pressure. Everyone thinks he did it.**

Me: **Yes, I agree. Everyone but the murderer that is.**

Derrik pushed the thought and Carlos signed at the same time: *You think he's innocent?*

**Of murdering his wife. Yes,** I thought and texted: **But he's rigid...and makes a good suspect.**

**Kellen and Zaria had nine kids. Unless he has another woman already lined up willing to take on that type of responsibility, I can't imagine he would divorce or kill his wife. It isn't logical.**

Carlos glanced towards Kellen's back and met my face. His hands were a bit shaky when he texted: **Whoever did it wants us to blame him.**

I nodded.

*But I'd like to see him go down.* Derrik thought.

I smiled. *Then find a way to give someone else the money.* "Would you go through the papers and see if there is a will? Or maybe look behind the paintings?"

"The paintings? You've seen too many movies. If it's here, it's in the safe."

"Do you need me anymore?" Ryan asked, leaning back on the cased opening.

"Not unless I find the missing organs," I said, still flipping through the items in the safe. "You can relax."

"We are not leaving our honored sister alone," Derrik said.

"Carlos is with me."

"And you aren't stupid enough to think I'd leave one of my progeny outnumbered."

I exchanged glances with Ryan. He looked like he might argue, but I had learned long ago after Derrik his set his mind to something, arguing about it just wasted time. Time we didn't have.

"No, I figured you'd stay," I said. "But I'm letting you know you don't have too. The witches are totally stoked to get to meet you and Pascaline."

"Well, Pascaline, at any rate." Derrik sighed, looking back into the living room where his wife was still chattering with the witches. "I hate these surprise public appearances. "Laurence is so much better at these situations than I am."

"Yeah, but Laurence would ditch early, and you won't," I said.

With an annoyed look at us both, Ryan went to go sit on the couch with the witches and Pascaline.

Derrik focused on the papers I had already retrieved. "This just looks like a rental agreement for the houseboat slip.

I was almost ready to start looking behind the artwork when I discovered another file folders squeezed into the back of the safe under another pile of cash: the deed to the houseboat and a copy of Zaria's will.

"Derrik, I found the will!" I handed it to him.

"I told you it'd be in the safe."

We glanced through it. The will was surprisingly ordinary.

"According to this, Zaria's kids get the houseboat and all the possessions within it as an inheritance split evenly. Kellen will manage it until they are twenty-one," Derrik said.

"After which, if one wants to buy the others out, it explains how to do that. And look there is a description of where to find the safe in the houseboat."

"Can I see that?" Kellen asked, calming.

"Of course," Derrik handed it to him.

Kellen scrolled the document. "Yes, this looks identical—or at least pretty close to the document—at home. I don't see anything different other than this is paper for air breathers."

*So money is not why Zaria died*, I thought to Derrik and texted the same words to Carlos.

*Too bad,* Derrik thought. *I would've loved to kill him.*

Carlos handed Derrik his notebook. Get in line.

Derrik looked between me and Carlos. Carlos took back the notebook.

No, I didn't read your mind. But, I can see what you're thinking.

"I'll try to be less obvious," Derrik said.

"Thank you," I said.

# Chapter 10

## 5:10 AM

---

I WASN'T SURE WHAT I WAS DOING, BUT recognized the need to question everyone further. I must figure out this puzzle. Maybe if I wanted to be a private detective, I ought to take forensic classes. I wondered if the Paper Flower Consortium Reeducation Grant would help pay for something like that.

Irving sat out on the deck, looking at the stars. Lost in his reverie, his gaze seemed far away and distant. Outside, it was easier to read his mind. Or his sorrow was so great that it broke through whatever spell dampened my skills. However the spell was still there. I could not read his thoughts.

I knelt in front of his chair. "You loved Zaria."

Irving lowered his gaze to meet my eyes. "You should be afraid of me, little vampire."

"Did she know?" I asked, ignoring his statement.

"She knew when we were young as you are," Irving said. "Then it didn't matter. She was married. I was married."

"But aren't you related?"

"Only by marriage," Irving said. "Not all in the pods are related by blood; that is a common misconception of outsiders. Culturally, our kind doesn't marry within our pod.

It might have been easier if I had gone to Lilianna's pod on the coast, but I couldn't bear to leave Elliot Bay. I wanted to hear Zaria's sweet song."

*A broken-hearted man might kill his love, but why, after so many years? Or maybe his wife had grown bitter?*

Irving didn't stop talking as he gazed out at the lake. "I told her to be careful when she took over this place. I told her it would only bring her to ruin. You should only have one house as it is the symbol of family love and home."

"Are you happy in your marriage?"

"Happy enough."

"But not like the wild love you had for Zaria?"

He chuckled. "Teenage girls are the same no matter what the species. You all think wild passions endure."

I didn't believe that, I had known love and loss. However, I was willing to let him think that I did.

"They don't?" I asked innocently wide-eyed.

"I have five kids. Lili is a good wife."

"My only goal here is to solve the murder so I can make $5000."

"Thank you for your honesty. I don't know if I am capable of wild love," Irving said. "If I were, I would have run away with Zaria when we were both young and foolish. She asked me once. Lili and I have many more things in common. It might seem strange to say, but we both loved Zaria. We both love our children, and our home is happy enough."

"Do you like Kellen?" I asked.

"Well enough."

"Even though he hit Zaria?"

Irving whole posture stiffened. He ran a palm over his

face. "Just between us, I hate the man." That was the truth. And now I knew his tells.

"I'm going to continue to question the others. Do you need anything?"

"Just not to be in that stuffy room. Those witches put something in the air, and I don't like how they touch us. Or you all for that matter. They have no shame."

"Do you want me to ask them to stop? If they don't listen to me, they will listen to Pascaline."

He closed his eyes and pinched his brow. "Do you really think your grandmother will try to help our people?"

"I don't see why she wouldn't. She loves helping kids. She said she gave Lilianna her information to pass on to the appropriate people."

"Good," Irving said. "The kids are going to need help after today. The loss of the podwife is a loss to the pod."

# Chapter 11

## 5:21 AM

I MOVED DOWN THE LADDER TO THE LOWER deck and checked my watch. Sunrise felt too close—especially since now Derrik, Pascaline, and Ryan were in danger of the sun too and we would have to go south.

Lilianna sighed and looked up from the magazine she was flipping through as I rounded the corner to the lower patio. "Have you solved the crime yet?"

The houseboat wasn't big enough that Lilianna hadn't heard Irving's words.

"No."

As I had never married, I didn't assume I knew what such a relationship was like. However, Derrik and Pascaline had both loved other people in their long marriage. It never stopped them from loving or at least being fond of each other. Perhaps Lilianna understood this as well. Perhaps love was not what she looked for in a marriage.

"Tick, tick. Only three hours to sun-up," Lilianna said. "I understand you feel you must question us, but Irving and I didn't do it."

"How do you know Irving didn't do it? You said you were making food all day and he was at work."

Lilianna's face hardened. Since I couldn't read the other woman's thoughts, I had to weigh her words prudently. I pulled another deck chair so I could sit across from the woman. I didn't like being so close to her talons, but in a business like mine, it helped to be vulnerable to get people talking. "I observed you weren't surprised by the safe."

Lilianna's lips spread into a smile, but it was still cold. "I like you, Norma. I supposed you figured out that Kellen and Zaria did not have a good marriage."

"Yes, Kellen said as much." I did not mention Irving as I wanted Lilianna to keep talking. "Would you say you and Zaria were close friends?"

"I suppose." Lilianna clicked her claws on the lawn chair's armrest.

"Did you know Zaria's plan for the money?"

"She didn't have a plan."

"She must have had an idea at least," I said. "What I need to know is: should I be looking for someone not on this houseboat?"

"Zaria was a beautiful person with a beautiful voice," Lilianna said softly. "But there were many discrepancies between Zaria's words and deeds."

That was an interesting way to say someone lied. "What type of discrepancies?"

"She never planned anything. She simply lied to Kellen about where she was. She'd say she was with me but wasn't," Lilianna said. "Most of the time, she was here."

"Do you think she was having an affair?" Norma asked.

"No. I think Zaria fantasied about an affair, but she

was surrounded by family too much of the time to have an affair. The pods are so close-knit. And someone who hates planning as much as Zaria would have found infidelity close to impossible."

"Then why go to a houseboat?"

Lilianna sighed and lifted herself. She slithered over to a panel in the wall and tapped it. Inside were crafting supplies, jam jars, silly romance novels and other things someone like Kellen might call trivialities.

"People sometimes want their own space. She loved her kids, but there was nine of them. I even think she still loved Kellen, but he is, was, a bad husband. He got physical. He never understood anything she did. He didn't try to understand. Then there were his affairs."

"His affairs? That's why he said paybacks a shark?" I asked.

"Yes. Kellen had multiple flings with shopgirls and the like. Zaria knew it. She was funneling money away from their accounts. She sometimes fantasized about leaving him, but was afraid of what might happen to her kids."

"Did it bother you she expected you to cover for her?"

"I got used to it. She was miserable," Lilianna said.

I didn't exactly trust she hadn't lied or exaggerated, but it was good to get insight.

"So you do you believe it was a poacher?"

"I have never seen a poacher on the coast or in Seattle," Lilianna said. "But then I had never met a vampire or a shade until tonight either. If I had to guess, I'd say Kellen killed her.

"Oh, he was sorry afterward, but he has a temper, that

one."

Our conversation was interrupted by shouting in the living room. I leaped to my feet and raced back inside. Lilianna glided in behind me.

# Chapter 12

## 5:29 AM

$\diamond$ ✦ $\diamond$

**F**OLLOWING THE COMMOTION AND HOPING the neighbors didn't call the cops, I dashed through the kitchen and back into the living room.

"Enough!" Kellen shouted, "She's my wife. I should drown all of you!" His undulating body snaked towards the three witches and my family.

With vampire celerity, Pascaline gently moved aside and ensured Ryan's safety. Bianca and Medea jumped back into a built-in. A vase fell and shattered into porcelain shards on the floor. Trying to not get hit by the shrapnel, Gwenna screamed as her leg was slashed. As chivalrous as ever, Derrik moved to catch the bleeding woman who started to swoon. He kept her head from cracking against the deck and her torso slipping into the spines of an angry merman. Carlos ran forward to put himself in between the injured women and Kellen.

Carlos's flesh ripped. Rotten blood spilled down his arm. He made a low guttural growl, that made every person stop moving, except me. I hurried to my friend and placed pressure on the injury.

He looked weak, but he wouldn't show his weakness.

"Hold the fort," I shouted at Derrik. "I've a first aid kit in the van!"

As fast as I was able, I hauled Carlos to the van holding him over my shoulders and his arm. I dumped him into the passenger seat. Seeing the injuring crushed my heart, but there were too many people to lose control. I took the surgical thread out of the first aid kit and sewed the flesh back into place. It felt strangely thickened, yet spongy.

And it hurt him. Carlos's scream shattered the night. Now I was sure someone would call the cops.

Samuel followed us. "I'm sorry. I'm sorry, Norma. Don't leave. That was an accident. Don't leave."

A few pieces of decomposed flesh loosened under my fingers. I wished I knew how to make Carlos live longer. The werewolf who accidentally made him had warned of rot. I wondered if I gave him a shot of my blood, but I was not sure of the effects. Sometimes we joked about him going all *Dawn of the Dead* on Seattle, but neither of us wanted to see it.

The old neighbor came out of his houseboat. "We're tired of this. We tried to be polite neighbors. Wait, how old are you?" The man blinked. "Holy...a merman? Where is Zaria? Are you that bore of a husband?"

*So her neighbors also knew of her unhappy marriage.*

"No, it's a great Halloween costume," I said quickly. I needed to dominate his mind, but sucked at domination. *Why couldn't Pascaline have followed me out?*

"Well, it's a little early for Halloween! I've lived on this lake for fifty years. You think I don't know a siren when I see one."

"I'm her cousin. We came looking for her," Samuel

said.

"Well, I haven't seen her since earlier today."

"And when was that, sir?" I asked.

"Oh, let's see, she was in their singing around one o'clock. Cleaning the houseboat or making jam I'd suppose. She tries to be a good neighbor, but sometimes her guests annoy us.

"Like you, girl, now shouldn't you be in bed? Where are your parents?"

"Actually my parents are inside. We're making the costumes for the costume parade."

I expanded my fangs and bit the inside of my cheek and let a bit of blood run down the edge of my lip. "See I'm a vampire, and my big brother is a zombie."

Carlos made a weak zombie sound.

*See us in costumes. See us in costumes.* I pressed into his mind over and over. *See us in costumes.*

"So you aren't partying?"

"No, sir. It's an all-night sewing party." A little more blood dribbled down my chin.

"Well, quiet down, or I'm going to call the cops. It's five o clock in the blessed morning! And then I'll have a word with Zaria about this sort of all-night party."

"We will, I promise."

The man shuffled away, grumbling.

*Sleep, sleep, sleep...go to sleep, and don't hear us again tonight.*

Samuel's mind rushed panicked thoughts towards her. "Your kinsman mentioned he is without work."

"He didn't get his last grant and been a bit depressed,"

I said. "He said, what work is there for a vampire marine biologist?"

"Would he work with us?" Samuel said earnestly.

*Was he trying to give me a reason to stay? Was that why he decided to pick up Derrik?* Merfolk and vampires were similar in their regard to family.

*Or is he looking for a reason to look like a nice guy?* Though I didn't quite believe my senses, I felt his fear, sorrow, and wanting someone to solve the crime. Samuel believed in me, Carlos, and Norma's Cleaning Service.

"You'd have to ask him. My honored brother doesn't like taking advice from me," I said.

"No one likes taking advice from their kid sister."

"I am the elder," I said hotly.

I identified Samuel's surprise without trying and in doing so I identified another tell.

"I'm not leaving. You can let everyone know." I handed Samuel a first aid kit. "Bring this in for Gwenna. I'm going to finish patching Carlos up."

Samuel glided back inside.

**Are you lying?** Carlos texted with one hand.

I wrapped the stitches in gauze. "We have family in there. And I have figured out a few things."

Carols: **What's that?**

"Like I said, they have some damping spell on the houseboat because I can't read anyone's mind in there or even in the patio. But here in the van, I could read Samuel well enough to know he is not the murderer."

Carlos: **Think one of the witches murdered that poor girl?**

"For the larynx. I don't know how to prove which one."

Carlos: **How do we break the spell?**

"By breaking whatever connection holds the witch's spell together," I said. "Here's what I know: Someone was here earlier than they claim today. That person had sex with a son of Poseidon. It may or may not have been Zaria herself.

"Then the witches came in to check in—they claim they did not see the body—before they left again, but I think they did...they are...

I looked into Carlos's face and pinched my lips together. I took a deep breath to collect my thoughts. "Something doesn't make sense about their story. I didn't travel a lot, but when you wrestled, you traveled a lot, right?"

Carlos nodded.

"Would you leave your bags in an open houseboat in the middle of the city with homeless people around?"

Carlos shook his head. **But some people are slobs.**

"Still one of the witches must have the key."

Carlos nodded and texted: **Find the key, find the voicebox, find the murderer?**

"That's what I'm thinking. Ready to go back in?"

Carlos nodded.

# Chapter 13

## 5:47 AM

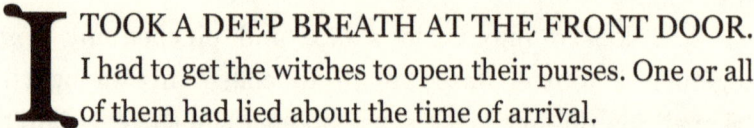

I TOOK A DEEP BREATH AT THE FRONT DOOR. I had to get the witches to open their purses. One or all of them had lied about the time of arrival.

I wondered if I should make a crazy announcement like people did in the movies, but what worked on film did not always work in real existence. I learned that the hard way. Still, I had an hour and twenty-one minutes before sunrise. I had to make it count. Derrik needed thirty minutes to get home. I must get someone to confess by no later than 6:30.

"I need to see everyone's keys," I said. "Whoever has the key to the front door met up with Zaria."

Bianca looked drowsy and half-drunk. Gwenna was still nervous about the whole affair, but Medea stood up straighter. A bit of sweat coated her brow. Her heart raced. I glanced at the other vampires who smiled, expanding their fangs. We couldn't read her mind, but any vampire who has lived a night could read the involuntary movements of her body.

"Why, dear, why is your heart racing so?" Pascaline asked. It was hard to pinpoint exactly how she faded her expression of a gentlewoman, but the angel of vengeance appeared in her place.

Medea started to tremble as Pascaline drew closer. She moved in front of the breadbox and stood there.

Moving quickly, I slid over to the breadbox. Behind it was another false panel. I reached for it.

Medea grabbed Bianca's purse and pulled out the anthame.

"Hey," Bianca cried and reached for Medea.

*Damn, damn, damn: why did I let Bianca enter the bunk room?*

Medea murmured the words to a spell in a language I did not understand, but the light flashed in front of my eyes. All I could see was brightness. I squinted and pressed my hands to my eyes, but the intensity wouldn't leave.

I felt for the counter.

"I'm blind. There is something in that panel, Medea doesn't want us to see!" *Why am I telling everyone what they already know?*

Carlos pushed his way to me. I smelled his familiar scent and slow heartbeat languidly thudding in his chest. I clutched at his coveralls, fearing I might tear into his fragile flesh.

"Assault is a criminal offense in Seattle," Derrik hissed. "Take it off of her, and I won't press charges."

"It's temporary," Medea said.

"What's in that panel?" I said.

"We're out. Carlos, bring along Norma if she doesn't come willingly," Derrik said.

Carlos's phone rang out: **I don't work for you.**

"Wait!" I cried, "Derrik, we must stay. Please stay.

Don't let them take whatever is in the panel." I decided to play a gambit. "It's Zaria's missing larynx."

Medea's mind shot open in terror. She screamed, "I didn't kill her! You aren't going to pin this on me!"

I felt the woman's panic and her innocence of the murder, but Medea knew who did it! She just didn't know she knew. *If I could just see a little deeper into her mind!*

My heart pounded. With all my might, I wished the light to stop scorching my eyes. All vampires fear the light. I focused on piecing more of the puzzle, but I was too slow. The sun would rise in less than an hour, and I was temporarily blinded.

"No, you didn't," I said, forcing my voice calm and hoping my expression looked the same. "You just helped cover it up and got the larynx as payment."

I felt the light creep over my face and wondered if I was wrong about the time. I was out in the sun. I would be burnt alive. Yet, I had been burnt before, even if I were dying, I would not show my terror. I had a reputation to keep.

I probed my mind towards Derrik. He was angry with my foolhardiness, but he was not sad or afraid. That meant I was not dying. *Even blind, I will solve this crime.*

I stated to the room, "I knew someone had to have been here because the witches came in the front door. Medea was here first—check she has the key."

"I was the last here!"

"No, you weren't," I said. "You claimed to have gotten bumped, but that's not true. You came early. Ran into the murderer and got a little fun between the sheets."

"Oh Medea, how could you?" Gwenna cried.

"Hush," Bianca said to Gwenna. "What are you going to do with our coven sister?"

"Take off the spell," Derrik repeated in his cool, calm vampire voice.

Medea screamed. Then ancient words thumped onto my eardrums as darkness flooded my sight. I could see again. The silver anthame clattered onto the counter. I blinked away the floaters out of my vision.

Medea was crying into her hands as Pascaline stood over her, digging her fingernails into her arm.

"How do your eyes feel, my lamb? Has your vampire sight returned?" Derrik asked, standing closer than I expected. His face was a mix of concern and rage. His pain for my pain was palatable. His progeny were the most important thing in his existence.

"I think so," I said still blinking.

"If your sight is at all damaged, I will file a lawsuit for lost income on behalf of the Paper Flower Consortium since blinding Norma affects not only my offspring, but her employees, and the coven as well," Derrik said.

I knew when Derrik was bluffing, but I doubted the witches did.

Medea stood very still. "I can't afford a lawsuit like that."

"Then I will sue your coven."

"The coven..." Bianca said, her pale face went nearly as gray as an ancient vampire.

"Then you better ensure your spell was cast correctly," Derrik said.

"It was. It was," Medea said.

Bianca moved closer to me. "May I see your eyes?" She looked deep within them. "They look clear."

I could read her fear written on her face. The three of them would likely be excommunicated if the Paper Flower Consortium brought on a lawsuit and they were connected with a siren's murder.

"What should we do with Medea for harming our honored sister?" Ryan asked, showing his fangs and letting his eyes flash red. To outsiders, Ryan could be terrifying when not looking like a professor.

"The vampires have no real authority here, but we can give you to the merfolk," Derrik said.

"They'll kill her!" Bianca screamed. "Don't do this. She just lost her temper for a moment. And the girl isn't hurt."

"Medea claims she did not kill Zaria," I began.

"I didn't!" Medea cried. "All right, All right! I came early. I told them I was bumped, but actually, I changed my flight weeks ago. There are some places—stores that sell interesting specimens and artifacts. Things my sisters get all judgey about!

"So I went shopping and mailed back my suitcase with what I had bought. That's why my backpack is all I have. I did not kill Zaria. I swear on the Great Goddess, I didn't!"

"But you don't mind desecrating a body for personal gain," I said.

"If Medea is guilty of body desecration, would you be happy with witch justice?" Derrik asked the children of Poseidon.

"What would that look like?" Kellen asked.

"Among our number, we have carried out coven

justice as much as that pains us to do so, the Seattle witches keep the same laws as this is international guidelines for all covens in America," Derrik said. "Am I correct in this?"

"Yes," Bianca said.

"I believe for body desecration some sort of binding spell is in order. Is that correct?"

"Yes."

"Do you have the power to turn her into an animal, for a certain amount of time," Derrik suggested.

The witches spoke amongst themselves. "Yes, we can do that, but Medea has the power to choose the form. And if that animal knows death or pain, she will return to her witch form immediately."

"I choose a cat," Medea said. "And only if Gwenna takes care of me."

"I'll take care of you," Gwenna agreed.

"Do you agree and will let the witches pass in peace?"

"Yes!" Irving shouted. "Turn her into a cat."

Once again, I felt his emotion were too big for the situation.

"How dare you!" Medea screamed. "I hooked up with you. I had the decency not to say anything in front of your wife, but how dare you judge me?"

I smiled. "Did you hook up with Medea after Zaria turned you down?"

"You, vampires, shut that kid up," Irving screamed.

"I am not a kid—and you aren't going to get out of this by shutting me up," I said. *But how can I get him to confess so the other merfolk would take him straight to their center of justice?*

"Okay, I admit it. I was here, but that doesn't mean I killed Zaria. The vampire is lying," Irving said.

There must be a clue. Something he said. I wracked my brain. The clam jam in the freezer. The recipe which was written out on the fridge. Samuel called it a secret recipe, but it was hardly a secret recipe if Zaria left it on the refrigerator. Irving jumped in when Lilianna made the snacks...

*Wait, but if Medea had the larynx, would Irving have taken the heart? Where would he have hidden it?*

Clam Jam was in the garbage disposal.

I reopened the freezer and looked at the jars of jam. One of the large party-sized jar's contents were not as all solid.

"Ryan, how big is a siren's heart?"

"Due to her age, I would guess about 290 grams," he replied.

"But how much volume would it take up?" I grabbed a pair of tongs from the utensil drawer. I lifted the jar out of the freezer. "Would it fit in this jar?"

"I guess so...yes."

Irving grabbed the anthame off the counter and swung it towards me. Though it was unnecessary, Pascaline pulled me away, faster than I could have moved. I might not be as quick as Pascaline, but on land, I was faster than any merman.

"What? I didn't kill her! You land-dwelling, little squid, your tentacles causing distrust between us, but you can't."

Lilianna cried, "Shut up! Irving, don't say another word. Even the lawyer, would tell you to keep silent. We saw how the vampires acted when that slut went after his kid, don't make this worse!"

So she knew or had already guessed.

"Tell him, Derrik, tell him to keep silent," Lilianna cried. "Don't let this idiocy destroy two families."

"That is true, you ought to keep silent when dealing with the authorities," Derrik said. "But we are not the authorities."

Everyone who wasn't merfolk covered their ears as a siren's call rang out from Kellen's mouth. "All of you shut up!"

Samuel grabbed Irving from behind, and Kellen pulled the knife from Irving's hand. "Irv, is this true? We were like brothers."

Irving gave his head a little shake. "No. You stopped being my brother the first time you hit your wife." His gaze narrowed at Kellen. As if in a trance he added, "I tried to protect her. I did. But she loved you. Even though you mistreated her, she always said 'Kellen is the father of my children.' "

Irving's lips spread. "I'll go to prison, but let his children know that he killed their mother's spirit. Let our whole community know what happened."

I pressed for information. "So what happened, Irving. I think we all know it wasn't premeditated."

"I came over for some party supplies. And I saw her stash.

"At first, I was happy. I thought Zaria had been saving money so we could leave together. We might start again in another pod. But no, it was for her and the kids to start again.

But I knew, if she left with the kids, Kellen would come after her. I tried to tell her that, but she wouldn't listen."

"There were already marks on her arms and neck. I just placed my hands where Kellen put his hands first. She was so tired of fighting. It was easy. She didn't even fight me off, she just cried.

"But she said, 'you're just like him' and I became so enraged I killed her. I loved her but I killed her."

"Is that why you took her heart?" Derrik asked.

"So he wouldn't have it," Irving hissed. "It would be mine again. Then Medea came in..."

"I haven't gotten this cleaned up enough," he said. "So I asked her what I had to give her to keep her mouth shut."

"I knew if I had a siren's voice, I would be able to dominate the witches of the coven to vote for me as their leader. And then I told him we needed to make love." Medea admitted.

"Why?"

"She said she wanted to hear me sing. I thought it was weird, but what the hell, she is a witch!"

"Sex magic," Bianca said with a sour look on her face.

"Explain slower," I said.

"Medea wanted to ensure Irving never talked about what happened. She knew what she was doing was wrong," Gwenna said. "Depending on the spell, he might not even remember it."

Bianca shook her head. "Tut tut tut."

"He performed well enough, but then he started to cry. Cry!" Medea said bitterly. "So I took his tears from him as well. If only the fool would have kept his mouth shut."

No one spoke right away. I wasn't even sure what to do with myself.

"So, now what?" Lilianna cried. Her voice was filled with such sorrow, it nearly broke my heart.

"We have no jurisdiction here," Derrik said. "I would suggest all of us land dwellers should prepare written statements which should suffice if we are subpoenaed. Then the children of Poseidon can escort their kinsman to their authorities."

Lilianna cried harder. Irving's face was so pale it was terrifying.

"Or find some other way to punish him within your pod," I said softly. "The vampires don't care and the witches don't want a scandal. It's up to you."

"Norma!" Samuel cried.

"There are nine kids without a mom. There are five kids who might lose their dad. What happens under the sea doesn't concern Norma's Cleaning Service or the Paper Flower Consortium."

"Is that all you care about?" Samuel screamed. "What about justice?"

"We're vampires," I said. "We punish our own within the coven system. Witches do the same. What you decide to do is ultimately up to you."

Kellen turned to me ready to rage.

I raised my chin in order to meet his eyes and said softly, "I lost my human mom when I was turned into a vampire. I almost didn't survive--I wouldn't have if it wasn't for Derrik and Pascaline. I sense Lilianna's fear for her kids."

"And I feel your fear for your kids."

Kellen crossed his arms. The rage was replaced by his real emotion: absolute terror of raising his children alone. I wasn't surprised. I had felt that emotion reflected back from Derrik a lot when I was a kid—and there was only one of me—not nine.

I turned to Samuel. "So, yeah, Sam, I don't care about justice when there are fourteen kids' lives on the line."

"The vampires' statements will support whatever the Children of Poseidon decide," Derrik said. "But you should know, Messrs Poseidonsons, I hate all who hurt those smaller than they...

Derrik was the most gentle of all vampires. Though most of the time he kept his rage locked away, he was not afraid to show just a hint of what lay in store for the guilty. What he wanted to do to a man who beat his wife. He never called it *street cred*, Derrik knew its value. "Be thankful, my wife and progeny have such a concern for your children, because it has been so long since I had seafood for supper.

"Seafood is good for the eyes," Pascaline added. "And our honored sister suffered a needless injury to hers."

"We will figure out something suitable, Derrik, or Irving will visit the authorities," Samuel said. "Thank you."

"I expect to hear back in a week," Derrik said.

# Chapter 14

## 6:37 AM

———◆◆◆———

KELLEN COUNTED OUT THE FIVE THOUSAND dollars from Zaria's stash. His expression showed how little he liked parting with any of the money, but at least he wasn't claiming he needed to make payments. "You earned this. Thank you."

Samuel tapped a loose fist against his heart. Lilianna said nothing. Irving had destroyed Zaria, her children, Lilianna, and their children. I didn't feel exactly good about my hand in that. Getting rid of bodies was good for the entire community, but someone always got hurt when solving a crime.

I walked my family to the car, I turned to Ryan. "You want cash?"

"Sure."

Vampires loved paper money. I counted out ten hundred-dollar bills and handed it to him. I glanced up at Derrik.

"Thanks for your help with the legal expertise," I said to Derrik.

He cut me off before I could offer him money. "I already told you what I want from you. Are you sure your eyes are better? And Carlos's arm?"

"I think so. I'll get both of us checked out with Agata tomorrow."

"Good."

Holding the fluffy cat-version of Medea in her right arm and dragging her suitcase with the other, Gwenna glanced back at the houseboat which Kellen locked up. "Well, now, where are we going to stay?"

"I lost my wife tonight and the man I considered my brother killed her," Kellen hissed. "Why are you bothering me about this?"

Gwenna scampered as far from Kellen as she could.

The merfolk ignored the landdwellers after that, slipped into the lake, and disappeared under the dark waters. I knew they headed west toward the Sound.

Bianca smiled at Pascaline shyly. "Could you help us?"

"The Paper Flower Consortium has the extended-stay hotel. The front desk has twenty-four-hour service," Pascaline said. "Norma and Ryan both carry phones in their pockets if you would like to inquire about a vacancy."

"I was hoping for a more friendly, intimate setting," Bianca said.

Pascaline was too composed to be shocked by an indiscreet question. "Forgive me, but I have no extra rooms in my home. My lady's maid lives in my second room, and I keep two thralls."

Derrik and Ryan said nothing.

Though Derrik also used the space for building matchstick models, he kept my old coffinroom pretty much the same as when I lived there. Ryan had a study with a hide-a-bed couch for the occasional guest. While vampires allowed anyone to come to Sabbaths, we did not open our homes to strangers.

Before the silence got weird, I stepped between Bianca and Pascaline, which ensured my family's escape to the car. "Carlos and I know of a haunted B&B outside the city."

"But we don't have transportation. That's why we are staying in the city."

"Well, Carlos and I can give you a ride over there, and they have an airport shuttle which also goes to Outlet Malls and Snoqualmie Falls."

Carlos: **And bus service**

He grabbed the pamphlet which the host had given him from the car and passed it to the Gwenna.

"It might not be the urban retreat you hoped for, but it is gorgeous, and they will accept Medea. And the ghost-in-residence makes an awesome chowder."

They agreed to let me call the B&B.

Carlos picked up their bags and carried them to the van. He adjusted the seats to make room for passengers.

"Aren't you afraid of the dawn?" Bianca asked, her tone was much sweeter than it had been earlier that night.

"Norma isn't afraid of anything much to the distress of our progenitor and Lady Pascaline." Ryan returned with Pascaline's beaded purse in his hands along with signed pictures of Pascaline for the three witches. "Give one to Medea after she turns back into a woman."

Gwenna handed Ryan her own card and pointed at her ear and mouth signaling: *call me.*

"And Pascaline said you mislaid your purse last time you visited."

There was something heavy inside. I could guess what was in the bag. Pascaline might appear to be the perfect vampire, the respectable lady, and wife of an attorney, but she was also an angel of vengeance and passion. She prioritized friendship and family above all else.

"Thank you for all your help, Ryan," I said.

"Be well. Don't stay out too long." He raised his eyes to the east.

"Carlos will drive, don't worry."

"Good. See you on Saturday evening."

"See you then." I waved at the car as Ryan turned away.

Piling into the passenger seat of my van, I rubbed my brow. I did not want to go to church services. However, if I was going to mentor an initiate, I ought to set a good example. Derrik and Ryan were church-going folk—as were most of the coven.

"You're lucky to be so close to your family," Gwenna said.

"Yes, I am lucky," I smiled to hide that I felt two ways. "Let's go. The fam's right; I need to watch the sun. Fortunately, we will be in the shade of the mountains by the time it rises."

"Do we have time to stop and get a litter box?" Gwenna asked.

"Yeah, there's a 24-hour drugstore on Mercer," I said. "It's big enough you should at least some cheap pet supplies there."

"You know, at first, I thought you were expensive and ripping us off, but you really are a full-service cleaner," Bianca said. "We will tell all our witch friends about you."

# Chapter 15

## 7:23 AM

$$\blacklozenge \blacklozenge \blacklozenge$$

THOUGH THE SUN HAD RISEN OVER THE Cascades and the sky was pink, Carlos turned into the valley of my birth and rebirth. He drove past my mother's old farm and turned onto a gravel drive still-marked with the rusty old mailbox which read CARUSO. I never changed the name on the mailbox as mail did not come to this address.

Only Derrik and the vampires who worked in the bank in 1963 knew I had purchased Bill's old hunting ground from the coven. Most of the other vampires wouldn't understand, and since I was the Shame of the Paper Flower Consortium, they would probably never ask me about it. After his execution, the coven seized Bill's assets. I had feared that if the need arose to liquidate the property, it would become a strip mall or a subdivision. Though the earth held some of my most terrifying memories, it also contained my rebirth, and the fun times Bill and I had together. The land also remembered Derrik who was once more joyful and carefree, before his First Born became ill.

In the 1980s, Derrik and I quietly fought to keep this strip of land zoned agricultural and won. With Tiger

Mountain to the east and Cougar Mountain to the west, the old hunting ground was a good place to think. Whatever Carlos thought about this land, he kept to himself.

Small cedars grew where the barn, which Bill used to run his experiments, used to stand. On the side of the drive, I had built a small shed and a firepit. Further into the wood, was an updated outhouse and a pump for the well.

Carlos parked the van in front of the firepit careful to turn the vehicle toward the west so no sun would come through the windshield.

I slathered on 100 SPF sunscreen and put on a wide-brimmed hat and sunglasses and a thick sweater, windbreaker, and gloves. I knew the risks and how to keep myself safe, but other vampires would not understand risking being burned alive by the sun for barbecue. I slipped the jar out of Pascaline's purse, tucked the bag in a cubby for safe keeping and put the jar in my jacket pocket.

Bill's ashes were mixed in with the dirt and gravel. He had been executed, but I could never stop wondering if he really died. The very idea seemed impossible. He had been a vampire who relished being a vampire and until his final death taught me to exist in the same way. In my heart, I knew my creator would have thought being a private detective would have been a cool job.

If I were able to change Fern, we would become connected. Fern would know about this place. Would Fern comprehend all that I felt for Bill? That I could love him because he was the first father I ever had known and hate him because he physically abused me? Would she love him too? *Or would Fern—like most other vampires--believe I am intrinsically broken?*

Carlos set up two folding lawn chairs. Then he climbed in the back of the van and changed out of the clothing he wore under his coveralls and put on a fresh pair of jeans and tee.

Enjoying the morning breeze, I sat in the shade of the van with a cooler of raw steak kabobs and poured cold drinks — water for Carlos, cow's blood for me.

Since there wasn't a burn ban this late in the year, I lit a small fire in the pit. I set the grate in place to get it hot for a good sear.

Carlos plopped down beside me.

Carlos: **I told you they'd be a pain.**

"You were right." I leaned my head back to watch the branches sway in the breeze and stretch my neck. The sound of pine boughs shifting above us brought me to a place of peace and comfort. They always did.

I pulled the jar from my pocket and handed it to him. "I thought we could see if Agata could put it in you."

Carlos: **Derrik knows you took that?**

"I dispose of bodies. I am disposing of this—what good is it going to do Zaria? I don't know if it would even work."

Carlos grumbled and spun the jar around in his hand studying the organ swimming in melting ice and some liquid.

"It's up to you."

Carlos set it very gently between icepacks and texted: **I have to think about it.**

I put the meat on the hot grate. The luscious smell of meat filled the air. At this moment, in the quiet, there were things that needed to be discussed. "Would you want to be private eyes for real?"

Carlos's words rang through his cellphone: I don't know how much longer I have.

I looked at him. "I don't want you to die." I wished my voice hadn't sound so childish.

His eyes softened. Neither do I, but I am going to rot sometime. Besides, Derrik's right. It's dangerous. Twice we've solved murders, and twice you've been hurt.

Holy Mother, I'm glad your family came tonight.

"I am too, though I wish they'd cut the endearments."

Carlos: Yeah. Good luck with that. Before my first death, my mother was still calling me Gordito and pinching my cheek whenever I came home.

Also it's funny to see Derrik act all vampirey. If I didn't know him I might have actually been scared.

I giggled, then grew serious again. "So I googled the requirements last month. We need to be eighteen or twenty-one to carry a gun. I don't carry a gun now, so I don't know why I'd want one. And it's pretty easy for me to look eighteen.

"Do you want a gun?"

Carlos: What? No! We're still going to be working for the community, right?

"Of course." I looked into the sky and watched the stars fade. "Let's see, what else? We are both US citizens, so that's not a problem. I need to properly license my firm and post a ten-thousand-dollar PI surety bond and get you a letter of employment. Then it's a couple of hundred-dollar licensing fees to the state of Washington and proof that we don't have criminal records that have anything to do with solving murders."

Carlos: **Whoa, you really looked into it?**

"The only thing is we need to be fingerprinted. It might get noticed that I am not aging, but the Paper Flower Consortium has been helping vampires "age" for over a hundred years.

"Derrik's right though. I do need to discuss this in depth with Jakub to ensure the finances work out. I mean the ten grand we were paid tonight is a lot of money, but once I account for gas, supplies, your paycheck and the autopsy I really don't know what I have left—especially if I end up missing a lot of work for services. Plus since we keep getting hurt, I figure you need hazard pay."

Carlos: **Are you trying to convince me or yourself?**

I picked up a piece of gravel and threw it towards the grass. "I don't know. Maybe I'm trying to think of what to say to Derrik. He doesn't want this for me, but then he didn't want the cleaning service for me either."

Carlos gave me a side-eye as he rotated the kabobs on the grate, wiped his hands on his jeans then texted: **What did he want for you?**

"To be a lawyer."

He laughed.

"Or work in the bank."

Carlos: **Something safe.**

"Yeah."

I changed the subject before I complained. It did no good to dwell on it. "So did you want to go to services with me next Saturday?"

Carlos: **Only if we're staying for the buffet. Oh, and can we not play Scrabble? Ryan always wins with all his** damn science words.

"I'll hide the board if I have to."

Carlos bumped my fist. Then started texting another message.

While I waited, I pressed on the meat with my fingers, testing for doneness. I took two kabobs off the flame and readjusted the others.

Carlos: **So solving murders would probably mean we wouldn't end up doing crappy jobs like helping ghosts move?**

"Not unless helping a ghost move solved a murder," I replied and passed him the first kabob.

He rose his meat towards me. His phone rang out: **What else am I going to do as I rot?**

I rose my kabob. "To the expansion of Norma's Cleaning Service."

He nodded his head once to show his agreement and tapped my kabob.

I expanded my fangs as I tore into the rare meat.

Carlos: **After dinner, let's carve the pumpkins. Who cares if they don't last, I never see trick or treaters in my building anyway.**

"Me neither," I said.

Carlos: **Besides someone always does something dumb on Halloween. We should have plenty of work.**

I set my empty skewer on the grate furthest from the flame and climbed back into the van to get the knives.

## The End

# Zaria's Clam Jam With Bacon

*Fancy folks and chefs might describe Clam Jam as a compound butter. The flavor is sort of like Clams Casino but there is no breadcrumbs or lemon. I have seen it used either a dip or as a topping for a protein or as a quick pasta sauce.*

- 1/2 pound bacon, 1 inch pieces
- 6 large shallots, minced (about 1 cup)
- 3 medium cloves garlic, minced
- Pinch red pepper flakes
- 1/4 cup dry white wine or stock
- 24 clams, purged and scrubbed
- 1 stick of butter       salt and pepper to taste

Bacon: In a large skillet or frying pan with lid, cook bacon over medium-high heat, stirring, until fat has rendered and bacon is browned and crisp, about 7 minutes. Lower heat if skillet gets too hot and begins to smoke.

Remove from heat and drain bacon. Reserve bacon fat.

Clams: Using bacon fat, stir in shallots, garlic, and red pepper flakes and cook, stirring, until shallots have softened, about 4 minutes.

Add wine or stock and clams, cover, and cook, checking occasionally, until the clams open. Using tongs, transfer opened clams to a large bowl to cool, continuing to cover pan and checking frequently for newly opened clams. Continue until last clams have opened. (Some may open only a crack; this is fine, just pry the shell fully open. If some refuse to open, discard.)

While the clams cool, uncover pan. Stir in butter, until wine and clam liquid have evaporated and the shallot-mixture has become jammy. Stir in the cooked bacon.

Remove from heat.

Working one at a time, pry off top shell of each clam and discard, making sure no shell fragments from hinge fall into clam. Dice.

In a medium bowl, stir shallot-bacon mixture and clams until thoroughly incorporated. Season lightly with salt and pepper.

Refrigerate immediately.

Hint: Clams can be salty, so be careful not to over-season.

# ABOUT THE AUTHOR

**M**UCH TO HER CHAGRIN, ELIZABETH Guizzetti discovered she was not a cyborg and growing up to be an otter would be impractical, so began writing stories at age twelve.

Three decades later, Guizzetti is an illustrator and author best known for her demon-poodle based comedy, *Out for Souls & Cookies*. She is also the creator of *For the Love of Pancakes, Faminelands* and *Lure* and collaborated with authors on several projects including *A is for Apex* and *The Prince of Artemis V*.

To explore a different aspect of her creativity, she writes science fiction and fantasy. Her debut novel, *Other Systems*, was a 2015 Finalist for the Canopus Award for excellence in Interstellar Fiction. Her short work has appeared in anthologies such as *Wee Folk and The Wise* and *Beyond the Hedge*.

She has always loved fantasy and horror books: especially vampires. A common theme in much of her work is questionable morality, the meaning of family, and people just trying to get through life whether they are elves, vampires, demon-dogs or humans.

This is why after writing *Immortal House*, Guizzetti went on a writing-spree of vampire books set in the Paper Flower Universe. She set the contemporary books in the series in Seattle because she resides there with her husband.

To follow her work, check out:
Twitter: @E_Guizzetti
Instagram: E_Guizzetti
Facebook Fan Page: Elizabeth.Guizzetti.Author
Webpage: http://elizabethguizzetti.com

PAPER FLOWER CONSORTIUM BOOKS:

## Norma's Cleaning Services Mysteries

Death Pulls a Stake Out, 2018
Death Hears a Siren, 2019
Death Sticks a Pixie, 2019

## Elders of the Paper Flower Consortium

Honor Among Vampires, 2019 (Agata's Story)
Chivalry Among Vampires, 2020 (Jakub's Story)
Accident Among Vampires Or What Would Dracula
Do?, 2021 (Norma's Childhood Story)
And more stories to come!

Immortal House, 2018 (Laurence's Story)
Vampires of the Paper Flower Consortium Anthology,
2022

## Vampires of the Paper Flower Consortium Podcast

is found on most podcatchers!

# OTHER BOOKS BY ELIZABETH GUIZZETTI

## Comics

*Faminelands*
*Out For Souls & Cookies!*
*Lure*
*For the Love of Pancakes*

## Novels and Novellas

*Other Systems*
*The Light Side of the Moon:*
*The Grove*
*Chronicles of the Martlet*
*The War Ender's Apprentice: Book 1*
*The Morality of a Necromancer: Book 2*
*The Assassin's Twisted Path: Book 3*

## Illustration Projects

*A is for Apex* written by Jennifer Brozek

*The Prince of Artemis V* written by Jennifer Brozek

# Prologue

## NOVEMBER 17, 1951

DEAR DIARY, HI. MY NAME IS NORMA MAE Rollins, and I don't want to die again. It hurt so much the first time.

I found you in my new desk in my new home. Vampires love to document everything. Their library holds many diaries. I'm pretty sure they will keep you if I fill you out. If they destroy me, I won't be forgotten.

I was born at home on February 8, 1938. I am fourteen, the only child of Margret Anne Rollins, née Rici, and her deceased husband, Robert Michael Joseph Rollins. I don't remember my real dad, but I loved my mom.

My vampire dad, Bill, plucked me from my life.

The Paper Flower Consortium in Seattle took me from Bill. I wish Bill told me more about the coven vampires. Before he faced execution, he had said, I needed to be strong, and no matter what, I must stay with Derrik, his progenitor.

For now, the coven agrees. I don't have a choice. The coven doesn't trust me. They think I'll break a pipe or something.

*Wait.* Maybe I shouldn't write it's my home.

It's Derrik's home.

He might not like if I claim it. I have to be careful until I figure what sets him off. I keep scrolling through films with vampires or rich, fancy people. None of it fits.

I don't know who I'm supposed to be here.

I admit Derrik's been pretty nice since we met tonight, but his bloody tears are chilling. His sorrow washes over me and I want to weep too. He loved Bill. Now he's stuck with me. I wish I could go home to my mom.

I guess I ought to start with the night I became a vampire.

*

# Chapter 1

## JUNE 21, 1951

DEAR DIARY, THE LAST NIGHT OF MY LIFE, I felt more alive than I ever had in my fourteen years. The stars twinkled above the grassy field outside Issaquah. The air was perfumed with summer grasses, pine, and fruit trees.

Careful I didn't interrupt Janice and Perry or Betty and Matt, I slowed my pace to let Teddy catch me. Every inch of skin felt alive as he squeezed my wrist. He playfully pulled me close. His lips tasted of beer and Wrigley's Doublemint gum as they brushed against mine. I wanted to kiss Teddy forever.

Still, our lips parted.

I giggled and darted away like the other girls did. The girls ran. The boys gave chase. I did the same. After all, one had to be careful not to ruin one's reputation.

Icy fingers, too big to be Teddy's, gripped my arms.

*The Fuzz,* I thought.

The sheriff would call Mom. I'd had a few sips of beer and smoked, but I wasn't blitzed. At worse, Mom would be "very disappointed" and give me extra chores.

My feet lifted from the ground. Wind bit the bare

flesh of my arms, legs, and face. Branches whipped past me in frenzied movement. Nothing made logical sense. I seemed to fly underneath the dark shape which held me.

I was dropped onto the concrete floor of somewhere cold that smelled of rotting meat and filth. A vampire's fangs loomed in front of me. *Vampires aren't supposed to be real!*

I screamed and struck my assailant with my flashlight. His pale lip split open and quickly stitched back together. He yanked the flashlight from my hand. I protected my throat with my arms, because in the movies, vampires always bite people in the throat.

He punched me.

Dazed, I fell backward into a metal table. He lifted me onto it and rolled me over. I spotted the pit half-filled with rotting bodies sprinkled with lime. Their mottled flesh twisted in bizarre angles. Cloudy eyes stared at the ceiling.

Wild with terror, I kicked out. I felt air.

I kicked again and again; I connected at least once. He grunted and leaned one hand on my back, pressing me into the metal. With his other hand, he ripped off my shoe and bobby-sock. His fangs pierced my heel. When he reopened his mouth, he whispered something about Achilles.

I tried to lift myself off the metal slab, but the vampire had me pinned. Cold leeched through my summer blouse. My muscles spasmed.

The barn spun. Darkness.

*No! Mom'll wake up ...*

*I won't be home ...*

*I'll be a rotting body covered in lye.*

He loosened his grip to check his stopwatch.

I twisted. With my free leg, I kicked the vampire as

hard as I could. Freed but light-headed, I sat and elbowed him in the chest. Agonizing pain radiated into my arm. Ignoring the throbbing, I punched him in his mouth, maybe his nose.

Blood sprayed onto my face. My eyes teared, burning with his fiery blood. My lips tasted like copper.

The vampire grabbed me.

With one final burst of strength, I lunged and clamped my teeth onto his hand. Salty, syrupy blood coated my mouth....